"I wan[t] [a second] chance[.]"

The teasing had left Evan's voice. "Do you?"

"Yes. Oh, yes," Mary Jo whispered.

"I love you," he said quietly. "Heaven knows, I tried not to.... When you told me you'd fallen in love with another man, I had no recourse but to accept that it was over."

A sob was trapped in her throat. This was the time to admit there'd never been another man, that it was all a lie....

"Can you tell me about him?"

"No!" She jerked her head from side to side in adamant refusal. She couldn't do it, just couldn't do it. She was continuing the lie, Lord help her, but telling him now would mean betraying his mother's part in all this. She *wouldn't* do it.

"Never mind." His arm cradled her shoulder, his grip tight. "We're getting married. Soon. And prepare yourself, sweetheart, because we're making up for lost time!"

Debbie Macomber was born in Washington State, where she still lives with her husband, Wayne, and youngest son, Dale, eighteen, and their dog, Peterkins. Her daughter Jenny, twenty-two, is married, and daughter Jody, twenty-three, is living and working in Seattle. Son Ted, twenty, is in the Army Airborne Rangers, and was recently married. Debbie's successful writing career started in childhood, when her brother copied—and sold!— her diary. She's gone on to a considerably wider readership since then, as a prolific and popular author published in several different romance series. She says she wrote her first book because she fell in love with Harlequin Romance novels—and wanted to write her own.

Debbie loves to hear from her readers. You can write to her at: P.O. Box 1458, Port Orchard, Washington 98366.

Books by Debbie Macomber

HARLEQUIN ROMANCE
3244—NORAH
3271—LONE STAR LOVIN'
3288—READY FOR ROMANCE

READY FOR MARRIAGE
Debbie Macomber

Harlequin Books

TORONTO • NEW YORK • LONDON
AMSTERDAM • PARIS • SYDNEY • HAMBURG
STOCKHOLM • ATHENS • TOKYO • MILAN
MADRID • WARSAW • BUDAPEST • AUCKLAND

Dedicated to
Carole Grande and her family
for their loving support
through the years

ISBN 0-373-03307-9

READY FOR MARRIAGE

Copyright © 1994 by Debbie Macomber.

Printed in U.S.A.

CHAPTER ONE

SHE COULD ALWAYS GROVEL at Evan's feet. Knowing him as well as she did, Mary Jo Summerhill figured he'd probably like that. The very fact that she'd made this appointment—and then had the courage to show up—proved how desperate she was. But she'd had no choice; her parents' future rested in her hands and she knew of no better attorney to help with this mess than Evan Dryden.

If he'd only *agree* to help her...

Generally, getting in touch with an old boyfriend wouldn't raise such anxiety, but Evan was more than just someone she'd dated a few times.

They'd been in love, deeply in love, and had planned to marry. In ways she had yet to fully appreciate, Mary Jo still loved him. Terminating their relationship had nearly devastated her.

And him.

Mary Jo wasn't proud of the way she'd ended it. Mailing him back the beautiful pearl engagement ring had been cowardly, but she'd known she couldn't tell him face-to-face. She should have realized Evan would never leave it at that. She'd been a fool to believe he'd take back the ring without confronting her.

He'd come to her angry and hurt, demanding an explanation. It quickly became apparent that he wouldn't accept the truth, and given no option, Mary Jo concocted a wild story about meeting another teacher and falling in love with him.

Telling such a bold-faced lie had magnified her guilt a hundredfold. But it was the only way she could make Evan believe her. The only way she could extricate herself from his life.

Her lie had worked beautifully, she noted with a twinge of pain. He'd recovered—just the way his mother had said he would. He hadn't wasted any time getting on with his life, either.

Within a matter of months he was dating again. Pictures of Evan, with Jessica Kellerman at his side, had appeared regularly in the newspaper society pages. Unable to resist knowing more, Mary Jo had researched the Kellerman family. Her investigation had told her everything she needed to know. Jessica would make the perfect Dryden wife. The Kellermans were wealthy and established, unlike the Summerhills, who didn't rate so much as a mention in Boston's social register.

Later the same year, Mary Jo had heard rumors of the extravagant Dryden family wedding. She been out of town that week at a teaching seminar, so she'd missed the newspaper coverage, but talk of the wedding and huge reception that followed had lingered for months. It was called the social event of the year.

That was nearly three years ago. Evan and Jessica were an old married couple by now. For all she knew, they might have already started a family. The twinge of regret became a knot in her stomach. Evan would make a wonderful father. They'd talked of a family, and she remembered how eager he was for children.

This wasn't exactly the best time for her to reenter his life, but she had no alternative. Her parents' future depended on Evan.

"Mr. Dryden will see you now," the receptionist said, breaking into Mary Jo's thoughts.

Her head shot up and she nearly lost her nerve right then and there. Her heart pounded furiously. In a dead panic she tightened her hold on her purse strap, fighting the urge to dash straight out of her chair and out of the office.

"If you'll come this way."

"Of course," Mary Jo managed, although the words came out in gurglelike sounds, as if she were submerged in ten feet of water.

She followed the receptionist down a wide, plush-carpeted hallway to Evan's office. His name was on the door, engraved on a gold plate. The receptionist ushered her in, and left.

Mary Jo recognized Evan's secretary immediately, although they'd never met. Mrs. Sterling was exactly the way he'd described her. Late middle-age. Short and slim, with the energy of a Tasmanian devil. Formidably efficient. He'd claimed that the woman could easily reorganize the world if she had to, and that she'd willingly take on any project he asked of her. She was loyal to a fault.

"Evan asked me to send you right in," Mrs. Sterling said, leading the way to the closed inner door. She opened it, then asked, "Can I get you a cup of coffee?" Her tone was friendly but unmistakably curious.

"No, thank you." Mary Jo stepped over the threshold, her heart in her throat. She wondered how she'd feel seeing Evan again after all this time. She'd already decided that a facade was necessary. She planned to approach him as if they were long-lost friends. Casual friends. With a smile, she'd shake his hand, inquire about Jessica and catch up on events in his life.

Now that only a few feet stood between her and the man she loved, Mary Jo found she couldn't move, barely even breathe.

Nothing, she realized, could have prepared her for the force of these emotions. Within seconds she was drowning in feelings she didn't know how to handle. She felt swamped and panicky, as if she were going down for the third time.

She conjured up Gary's face, the man she'd dated off and on for the past few months, but that didn't help. Next she struggled to come up with some clever comment, some joke, anything. Instead, all she could remember was that the man she'd loved three years ago, loved now, was married to someone else.

Evan sat at his desk, writing; only now did he look up. Their eyes met and for the briefest moment, he seemed to experience the same sense of loss and regret she was feeling. He blinked and the emotion disappeared, wiped out with a mere movement of his eyes.

"Hello, Evan," she said, amazed at how casual she sounded. "I imagine it's a surprise to see me after all this time."

He stood and extended his hand for a perfunctory shake, and when he spoke his voice was crisp and professional. "Mary Jo. It's good to see you."

Mary Jo nearly laughed out loud. Evan never did know how to tell a good lie. He was anything but pleased to see her again.

He motioned toward the chair on the other side of his desk. "Sit down."

She did, gratefully, uncertain how much longer her knees would support her. She set her purse on the carpet and waited for her heart rate to return to normal before she told him the purpose of her visit.

"Did Mary offer you a cup of coffee?"

"Yes. I'm fine, thank you," she said hurriedly. Her hands were trembling.

Evan sat down again and waited.

"I—guess you're wondering why I'm here...."

He leaned back in his chair, looking cool and composed. It'd been three long years since she'd last seen him. He hadn't changed, at least not outwardly. He remained one of the handsomest men she'd ever seen. His hair was as dark as his eyes, the color of rich Swiss chocolate. His features were well defined, almost chiseled, but that was too harsh a word for the finely cut, yet pronounced lines of his face. Walter Dryden, Evan's father, was a Massachusetts senator, and it was commonly accepted that Evan would one day enter politics himself. He certainly had the smooth, clean-cut good looks for such a calling.

What had made him fall in love with Mary Jo? She'd always wondered, always been fascinated by that question. She suspected it had something to do with being different from the other women he'd dated. She'd amused him, hadn't taken him too seriously, made him laugh.

"You have something you wanted to discuss with me?" he prompted, his tone revealing the slightest hint of irritation.

"Yes...sorry," she said, quickly returning her attention to the matter at hand. "My parents... actually, my father...he retired not long ago," she said, rushing the words together, "and he invested his savings with a financial company, Adison Investments. Have you ever heard of the firm?"

"No, I can't say that I have."

This didn't surprise Mary Jo. Wealthy men like Evan had huge financial portfolios with varied and multiple investments. Her father had taken his life's savings and entrusted it to a man he'd met and trusted completely.

"Dad invested everything he had with the company," she continued. "According to the terms of the agreement, he was to receive monthly interest checks. He hasn't. At first there were a number of plausible excuses, which Dad readily accepted. He wanted to believe this Bill Adison so much that it was easier to accept the excuses than face the truth."

"Which is?" Evan asked.

"I...I don't know. That's why I'm here. My father's worked thirty-five years as a construction electrician. He's raised six children, scrimped and saved all that time to put something extra away for his retirement. He wanted to be able to travel with Mom. They've dreamed of touring the South Pacific, and now I'm afraid they're going to be cheated out of everything."

Evan scribbled down a few notes.

"I'm coming to you because I'm afraid my brothers are about to take things into their own hands. Jack and Rich went to Adison's office last week and made such a fuss they were almost arrested. It'd destroy my parents if my brothers ended up in jail over this. As far as I can see, the only way to handle it is through an attorney."

Evan made another note. "Did you bring the papers your father signed?"

"No. I didn't tell anyone I was coming to see you. I thought if I could convince you to accept this case for my family, I'd bring my parents in and you could discuss the details with them. You need to understand that it's more than the money. My dad's embarrassed that he could have trusted such a man. He feels like an old fool." Her father had become very depressed. Adison Investments had robbed him of far more than his retirement savings. They'd taken his self-confidence and left him feeling vulnerable and inept.

"There are strict laws governing investments in this state."

Anxious to hear what he had to say, Mary Jo leaned forward in her chair. This was the very reason she'd swallowed her pride and come to Evan. He had the knowledge and political clout to be effective in ways her family never could.

"Then you can help us?" she asked eagerly. Evan's hesitation sent her heart plummeting. "I'll be happy to pay you whatever your fee is," she added, as if that was his sole concern. "I wouldn't expect you to charge less than you'd receive from anyone else."

Evan stood and walked over to the window, his back to her. "Our firm specializes in corporate law."

"That doesn't mean you can't take this case, does it?"

Evan clenched his hands at his sides, then flexed his fingers. "No, but these sorts of cases have a tendency to become involved. You may end up having to sue."

"My family is willing to do whatever to takes to settle this matter," she said with a stubborn tilt to her jaw.

"Lawsuits don't come cheap," he warned, turning around to face her.

"I don't care and neither do my brothers. True, they don't know I made an appointment to see you, but once I tell them, I'm sure they'll be willing to chip in whatever they can to cover your fee." They wouldn't be able to afford much. Mary Jo was the youngest of six and the only girl. Her brothers were all married and raising young families. There never seemed to be enough money to go around. The burden of the expense would fall on her shoulders, but Mary Jo readily accepted that.

"You're sure you want me to handle this?" Evan asked, frowning.

"Positive. There isn't anyone I trust more," she said simply. Her eyes met his and she refused to look away.

"I could recommend another attorney, someone far more qualified in the area of investment fraud—"

"No," she broke in. "I don't trust anyone but you." She hadn't meant to tell him that and, embarrassed, quickly lowered her gaze.

He didn't say anything for what seemed like a very long time. Mary Jo held her breath, waiting. If he expected her to plead, she'd do it willingly. It was fair compensation for the appalling way she'd treated him. "Please," she added, her voice low and trembling.

Evan's shoulders lifted with a drawn-out sigh. "Before I decide, fill me in on what you've been doing for the past three years."

Mary Jo hadn't anticipated this, wasn't prepared to detail her life. "I'm still teaching."

"Kindergarten?"

"Yes," she said enthusiastically. She loved her job. "Five-year-olds are still my favorites."

"I notice you're not wearing a wedding band."

Her gaze automatically fell to her ring finger, and she pinched her lips tightly together.

"So you didn't marry lover boy, after all."

"No."

"What happened?" he asked. He seemed almost to enjoy questioning her. Mary Jo felt as though she were on the witness stand being cross-examined.

She shrugged, not wanting to become trapped in a growing web of untruths. She'd regretted that stupid lie every day for the past three years.

"It didn't work out?" he suggested.

This was agony for her. "You're right. It didn't work out."

He grinned then, for the first time, as if this information delighted him.

"Are you seeing someone now?"

"I don't believe that information's necessary to the case. You're my attorney, not my confessor."

"I'm nothing to you," he said and his words were sharp. "At least not yet."

"Will you take the case or won't you?" she demanded.

"I haven't decided yet."

He did want her to grovel. And they said hell hath no fury like a *woman* scorned. Apparently women didn't hold the patent on that.

"Gary Copeland," she said stiffly, without emotion. "Gary and I've been seeing each other for several months."

"Another teacher?"

"He's a fireman."

Evan nodded thoughtfully.

"Will you or won't you help my parents?" she asked again, growing tired of this silly game.

He was silent for a moment, then said abruptly, "All right. I'll make some inquiries and learn what I can about Adison Investments."

Mary Jo was so relieved and grateful she sagged in her chair.

"Make an appointment with Mrs. Sterling for next week, and bring your father in with you. Friday would be best. I'll be in court most of the week."

"Thank you, Evan," she whispered, blinking rapidly in an effort to fight back tears.

She stood, eager now to escape. Resisting the urge to hug him, she hurried out of his office, past Mrs. Sterling and into the hallway. She was in such a blind rush she nearly collided with a woman holding a toddler in her arms.

"Oh, I'm so sorry," Mary Jo said, catching herself. "I'm afraid I wasn't watching where I was going."

"No problem," the other woman said with a friendly smile. She held the child protectively against her hip. The little boy, dressed in a blue-and-white sailor suit, looked up at her with eyes that were dark and solemn. Dark as rich Swiss chocolate.

Evan's eyes.

Mary Jo stared at the tall lovely woman. This was Jessica, Evan's wife, and the baby in her arms was Evan's son. The flash of pain nearly paralyzed her.

"I shouldn't have been standing so close to the door," Jessica went on to say. "My husband insisted he was taking us to lunch, and asked me to meet him here."

"You must be Jessica Dryden," Mary Jo said, finding the strength to offer her a genuine smile. She couldn't take her eyes off Evan's son. He now wore a cheerful grin and waved small chubby arms. If circumstances had been different, this child might have been her own. The void inside her widened; she'd never felt so bleak, so empty.

"This is Andy." Jessica did a small curtsy with her son in her arms.

"Hello, Andy." Mary Jo gave him her hand, and like a proper gentleman, he took it and promptly tried to place it in his mouth.

Jessica laughed softly. "I'm afraid he's teething. Everything goes to his mouth first." She walked with Mary Jo toward the exit, bouncing the impatient toddler against her hip. "You look familiar," she said casually. " Do I know you?"

"I don't think so. My name's Mary Jo Summerhill."

Jessica's face went blank, then recognition swept into her eyes as her smile slowly evaporated. Any censure, however, was quickly disguised.

"It was nice meeting you," Mary Jo said quickly, speeding up as they neared the door.

"Evan's mentioned you," Jessica said.

Mary Jo stopped suddenly. "He has?" She couldn't help it. Curiosity got the better of her.

"Yes. He . . . thought very highly of you."

That Jessica used the past tense didn't escape Mary Jo. "He's a top-notch attorney."

"He's wonderful," Jessica agreed. "By the way, I understand we have a mutual friend. Earl Kress."

Earl had been a volunteer at Mary Jo's school. He'd tutored slow readers, and she'd admired his patience and persistence, and especially his sense of humor. The children loved him.

Earl mentioned Evan's name at every opportunity. He seemed to idolize Evan for taking on his civil suit against the school district—and winning.

Earl had graduated from high school functionally illiterate. Because he was a talented athlete, he'd been passed from one grade to the next. Sports were important to the schools, and the teachers were coerced into giving him passing grades. Earl had been awarded a full-ride college scholarship but suffered a serious knee injury in football training camp two weeks after he arrived. Within a couple of months, he'd flunked out of college. In a landmark case, Earl had sued the school district for his education. Evan had been his attorney.

The case had been in the headlines for weeks. During the trial, Mary Jo had been glued to the television every night, anxious for news. As a teacher, she was, of course, concerned with this kind of crucial education issue. But in all honesty, her interest had less to do with Earl Kress than with Evan. Following the case gave her the opportunity to see him again, even if it was only on a television screen and for a minute or two at a time.

She'd cheered when she heard that Earl had won his case.

In the kind of irony that life sometimes tosses, Mary Jo met Earl about a year later. He was attending college classes and volunteering part-time as a tutor at the grade school. They'd become quick friends. She admired the young man and missed him now that he'd returned to the same university where he'd once failed. Again he'd gone on a scholarship, but this time it was an academic one.

"Yes, I know Earl," Mary Jo said.

"He mentioned working with you to Evan. We were surprised to learn you weren't married."

Evan knew! He'd made her squirm and forced her to tell him the truth when all along he'd been perfectly aware that she was still single. Mary Jo's hands knotted at her sides. He'd taken a little too much delight in squeezing the information out of her.

"Darling," a husky male voice said from behind Mary Jo. "I hope I didn't keep you waiting long." He walked over to Jessica, lifted Andy out of her arms and kissed her on the cheek.

Mary Jo's jaw fell open as she stared at the couple.

"Have you met my husband?" Jessica asked. "Damian, this is Mary Jo Summerhill."

"How...hello." Mary Jo was so flustered she could barely think.

Evan wasn't married to Jessica. His *brother* was.

CHAPTER TWO

"CAN YOU HELP US?" Norman Summerhill asked Evan anxiously.

Mary Jo had brought both her parents. Evan was reading over the agreement her father had signed with Adison Investments. With a sick feeling in the pit of her stomach, she noticed he was frowning. The frown deepened the longer he read.

"What's wrong?" Mary Jo asked.

Her mother hands were clenched so tightly that her fingers were white. Financial affairs confused and upset Marianna Summerhill. From the time Marianna had married Norman, she'd been a housewife and mother, leaving the financial details of their lives to her husband.

Mary Jo was fiercely proud of her family. Her father might not be a United States senator, but he was an honest and honorable man. He'd dedicated his life to his wife and family, and worked hard through the years to provide for them. Mary Jo had been raised firmly rooted in her parents' love for each other and for their children.

Although close to sixty, her mother remained a beautiful woman, inside and out. Mary Jo had inherited her dark hair and brown eyes and her petite five-foot-four-inch frame. But the prominent high cheekbones and square jaw were undeniably from her father's side of the family. Her brothers towered above her and, like her parents, were delighted their youngest sibling was a girl.

That affection was returned. Mary Jo adored her older brothers, but she knew them and their quirks and foibles well. Living with five boys—all very different personalities—had given her plenty of practice in deciphering the male psyche. Evan might have come from a rich, upper-crust family, but he was a man, and she'd been able to read him like a book from the first. She believed that her ability to see through his playboy facade was what had originally attracted her to him. That attraction had grown and blossomed until...

"Come by for Sunday dinner. We eat about three, and we'd enjoy getting to know you better," her mother was saying. "It'd be an honor to have you at our table."

The words cut into Mary Jo's thoughts like a scythe through wheat. "I'm sure Evan's too busy for that, Mother," she blurted out.

"I appreciate the invitation," Evan said, ignoring Mary Jo.

"You're welcome to stop off at the house any time you like, young man," her father added, sending his daughter a glare of disapproval.

"Thank you. I'll keep it in mind," Evan said absently as he returned his attention to the investment papers. "If you don't object, I'd like an attorney friend of mine to read this over. I should have an answer for you in the next week or so."

Her father nodded. "You do whatever you think is necessary. And don't you worry about your fee."

"Dad, I already told you! I've talked to Evan about that. This is my gift to you."

"Nonsense," her father argued, scowling. "I was the one who was fool enough to trust this shyster. If anyone pays Evan's fee, it'll be me."

"We don't need to worry about that right now," Evan interjected smoothly. "We'll work out the details of my bill later."

"That sounds fair to me." Norman Summerhill was quick to agree, obviously eager to put the subject behind him. Her father had carried his own weight all his life and wouldn't take kindly to Mary Jo's accepting responsibility for this debt. She hoped she could find a means of doing so without damaging his formidable pride.

"Thank you for your time," she said to Evan, desperate to be on her way.

"It was good to see you again, young man," Norman said expansively, shaking hands with Evan. "No need to make yourself scarce. You're welcome for dinner any Sunday of the year."

"Daddy, please," Mary Jo groaned under her breath. The last thing she wanted was to have Evan show up for Sunday dinner with her five brothers and their assorted families. He wasn't accustomed to all the noise and chatter that invariably went on during meals. Her one dinner with his family had sufficiently pointed out the glaring differences between their upbringings.

"Before you leave," Evan said to Mary Jo, "my brother asked me to give you this. I believe it's from Jessica." He handed her a sealed envelope.

"Thank you," Mary Jo mumbled. For the better part of their meeting, he'd avoiding speaking to her. He hadn't been rude or tactless, just businesslike and distant. At least toward her. With her parents, he'd been warm and gracious. She doubted they'd even recognized the subtle difference between how he treated them and how he treated her.

MARY JO DIDN'T OPEN the envelope until after she'd arrived back at her cozy duplex apartment. She stared at it several moments, wondering what Jessica Dryden could possibly have to say to her.

No need to guess, she decided, and tore open the envelope.

Dear Mary Jo,
I just wanted you to know how much I enjoyed meeting you. When I asked Evan why you were in to see him, he clammed right up. I should have known better—prying information out of Evan is even more difficult than it is with Damian.

From your reaction the other day, I could tell you assumed I was married to Evan. Damian and I got quite a chuckle out of that. You see, just about everyone tried to match me up with Evan, but I only had eyes for Damian. If you're free some afternoon, give me a call. Perhaps we could have lunch.

Warmest regards,
Jessica

Jessica had written her telephone number beneath her signature.

Mary Jo couldn't understand why Damian's wife would seek her out. They were virtual strangers. Perhaps Jessica knew something Mary Jo didn't—something about Evan. The only way to find out was to call.

Although Mary Jo wasn't entirely sure she was doing the right thing, she reached for the phone.

Jessica Dryden answered almost immediately.

"Mary Jo! Oh, I'm so glad to hear from you," she said immediately. "I wondered what you'd think about my note. I don't usually do that sort of thing, but I was just so delighted you'd been to see Evan."

"You said he's mentioned me?"

"A number of times. Look, why don't you come over one afternoon soon and we can talk? You're not teaching right now, are you?"

"School let out a week ago," Mary Jo concurred.

"That's what I thought. Could you stop by next week? I'd really enjoy talking to you."

Mary Jo hesitated. Her first introduction to Evan's family had been a catastrophe, and she'd come away knowing their love didn't stand a chance. A second sortie might prove equally disastrous.

"I'd like that very much," Mary Jo found herself saying. If Evan had been talking about her, she wanted to know what he'd said.

"Great. How about next Tuesday afternoon? Come for lunch and we can sit on the patio and have a nice long chat."

"That sounds great," Mary Jo said.

It wasn't until later that evening, when she was filling a croissant with a curried shrimp mixture for dinner, that Mary Jo stopped to wonder exactly *why* Jessica was so eager to "chat" with her.

SHE LIKED GARY. She really did. Though why she felt it was necessary to remind herself of this, she didn't know. She didn't even *want* to know.

It had been like this from the moment she'd broken off her relationship with Evan. She'd found fault with every man she'd dated. No matter how attractive he was. Or how successful. How witty, how considerate...it didn't matter.

Gary was very *nice,* she repeated to herself.

Unfortunately he bored her to tears. He talked about his golf game, his bowling score and his prowess on the handball court. Never anything that was important to her. But his biggest fault, she'd realized early on in their relationship was that he wasn't Evan.

They'd dated infrequently since the beginning of the year. To be honest, Mary Jo was beginning to think that, to Gary, her biggest attraction was her mother's cooking. Invariably, Gary stopped by early Sunday afternoon, just as she was about to leave for her parents' home. It'd happened three out of the past five weeks. She strongly suspected he'd been on duty at the fire hall the two weeks he'd missed.

"You look especially lovely this afternoon," he said when she opened her front door to him now. He held out a bouquet of pink carnations, which she took with a smile, pleased by his thoughtfulness.

"Hello, Gary."

He kissed her cheek, but it seemed perfunctory, as if he felt some display of affection was expected of him. "How've you been?" he muttered, easing himself into the old rocking chair next to the fireplace.

Although Mary Jo's rooms were small, she'd thoughtfully and carefully decorated each one. The living room had an Early American look. Her brother Lonny, who did beautiful woodwork, had carved her an eagle for Christmas, which she'd hung above the fireplace. In addition to her rocking chair, she had a small sofa and an old oak chest that she'd restored herself. Her mother had crocheted an afghan for the back of the sofa in a patriotic blend of red, white and blue.

Her kitchen was little more than a wide hallway that led to a compact dining space in a window alcove. Mary Jo loved to sit there in the morning sunshine with a cup of coffee and a book.

"You're lucky, you know," Gary said, looking around as if seeing the room for the first time.

"How do you mean?"

"Well, first off, you don't have to work in the summer."

This was an old argument and Mary Jo was tired of hearing it. True, school wasn't in session for those two and a half months, she didn't spend them lolling on a beach. This was the first time in years that she wasn't attending courses to upgrade her skills.

"You've got the time you need to fix up this place the way you want it," he went on. "You have real decorating talent, you know. My place is a mess, but then I'm only there three or four days out of the week, if that."

If he was hinting that he'd like her to help him decorate his place, she refused to take the bait.

"Are you going over to your parents' this afternoon?" Gary asked cheerfully. "I don't mean to horn in, but your family doesn't seem to mind, and the two of us have an understanding, don't we?"

"An understanding?" This was news to Mary Jo.

"Yeah. We're... I don't know, going together I guess."

"I thought we were friends." That was all Mary Jo intended the relationship to be.

"Just friends." Gary's face fell. His gaze wandered to the carnations he'd brought with him.

"When was the last time we went out on a date?" she asked, crossing her arms. "A real date."

"You mean to the movies or something?"

"Sure." Surveying her own memory, she could almost count one hand the number of times he'd actually spent money taking her out. The carnations were an exception.

"We went to the Red Sox game, remember?"

"That was in April," she reminded him.

Gary frowned. "That long ago? Time certainly flies, doesn't it?"

"It sure does."

Gary rubbed his face. "You're right, Mary Jo. I've taken you for granted, haven't I?"

She was about to say they really didn't have much of an understanding, after all, did they. Yet a serious relationship with Gary didn't interest her and, difficult as it was to admit now, never had. She'd used him to block out the loneliness. She'd used him so her parents wouldn't worry about her. They firmly believed that a woman, especially a young woman, needed a man in her life, so she'd trotted out Gary in order to keep the peace. She wasn't exactly proud of her motives.

Gary reached for her hand. "How about a movie this afternoon?" he suggested contritely. "We'll leave right after dinner at your parents'. We can invite anyone who wants to come along, as well. You wouldn't mind, would you?"

Gary was honestly trying. He couldn't help it that he wasn't Evan Dryden. The thought slipped uncensored into her mind.

"A movie sounds like a great idea," she said firmly. She was going, and furthermore, she was determined to have a wonderful time. Just because Evan Dryden had briefly reentered her life was no reason to wallow in the impossible. He was way out of her league.

"Great." A smile lighted his boyish face. "Let's drive on over to your mom and dad's place now."

"All right," Mary Jo said. She felt better already. Her relationship with Gary wasn't ideal—it wasn't even close to ideal—but he was her friend. Love and marriage had been built on a whole lot less.

Before they left the house, Gary reached for the bouquet of carnations. Mary Jo blinked in surprise, and he hesitated, looking mildly chagrined. "I thought we'd give these to your mother. You don't mind, do you?"

"Of course not," she mumbled, but she did, just a little.

Gary must have realized it because he added, "Next time I'll bring some just for you."

"You owe me one, fellow."

He laughed good-naturedly and with an elaborate display of courtesy, opened the car door for her.

Mary Jo slid into the seat and snapped her seat belt into place. During the brief drive to her parents' house, less than two miles away she and Gary didn't speak; instead, they listened companionably to part of a Red Sox game.

Her nephews and nieces were out in the huge side yard, playing a rousing game of volleyball when they arrived. Gary parked his car behind her oldest brother's station wagon.

"I get a kick out of how much fun your family has together," he said a bit wistfully.

"We have our share of squabbles, too." But any disagreement was rare and quickly resolved. Three of her brothers, Jack, Rich and Lonny, were construction electricians like their father. Bill and Mark had both become mechanics and had opened a shop together. They were still struggling to get on their feet financially, but both worked hard. With time, they'd make a go of it; Mary Jo was convinced of that.

"I wonder what your mother decided to cook today," Gary mused, and Mary Jo swore he all but licked his chops.

Briefly she wondered if Gary bothered to eat during the week, or if he stored up his appetite for Sunday dinners with her family.

"I've been introduced to all your brothers, haven't I?" he asked, frowning slightly as he helped her out of the car.

Mary Jo had to think about that. He must have been. Not every brother came every Sunday, but over the course of the past few months surely Gary had met each of her five brothers.

"I don't recognize the guy in the red sweatshirt," he said as they moved up the walk toward the house.

Mary Jo was distracted from answering by her mother, who came rushing down the porch steps, holding out her arms as if it'd been weeks since they'd last seen each other. She wore an apron and a smile that sparkled with delight. "Mary Jo! I'm so glad you're here." She hugged her daughter close for a long moment, then turned toward Gary.

"How sweet," she said, taking the bouquet of carnations and kissing his cheek.

Still smiling, Marianna gestured her attention to her daughter. "You'll never guess who stopped by!"

It was then that Mary Jo noticed Evan walking toward them. Dressed in jeans and a red sweatshirt, he carried Lenny, her six year old nephew, tucked under one arm, and Robby, his older brother by a year, under the other. Both boys were kicking and laughing.

Evan stopped abruptly when he saw Mary Jo and Gary. The laughter drained out of his eyes.

"Hello," Gary said, stepping forward. "You must be one of Mary Jo's brothers. I don't believe we've met. I'm Gary Copeland."

CHAPTER THREE

"WHAT ARE YOU *doing* here?" Mary Jo demanded the minute she could get Evan alone. With a house full of people, it had taken her the better part of two hours to corner him. As it was, they were standing in the hallway and could be interrupted at any moment.

"If you'll recall, your mother invited me."

"The only reason you're here is to embarrass me." The entire meal had been an exercise in frustration for Mary Jo. Evan had been the center of attention and had answered a multitude of questions from her parents and brothers. As for the way he'd treated Gary— every time she thought about it, she seethed. Anyone watching them would think Evan and Gary were old pals. Evan had joked and teased with Gary, even going so far as to mention that Mary Jo's ears grew red whenever she was uncomfortable with a subject.

The second he'd said it, she felt the blood rush to her ears. Soon they were so hot she was afraid Gary might mistake them for a fire engine.

What upset her most was the way Evan had her family eating out of his hand. Everyone acted as though he was some sort of celebrity! Her mother had offered him the first slice of chocolate cake, something Mary Jo could never remember happening. No matter who was seated at the dinner table, her father had always been served first.

"I didn't mean to make you uncomfortable," Evan said now, his eyes as innocent as a preschooler's.

Mary Jo wasn't fooled. She knew why he'd come—to humiliate her in front of her family. Rarely had she been angrier. Rarely had she felt more frustrated. Tears filled her eyes and blurred her vision.

"You can think what you want of me, but don't *ever* laugh at my family," she said between gritted teeth. She whirled away and had taken all of two steps when he caught hold of her shoulder and yanked her around.

Now he was just as angry. His dark eyes burned with it. They glared at each other, faces tight, hands clenched.

"I would never laugh at your family," he said evenly.

Mary Jo straightened her shoulders defiantly. "But you look forward to make a laughingstock out of *me*. Let me give you an example. You knew I wasn't married, yet you manipulated me into admitting it. You *enjoy* making me uncomfortable!"

He grinned then, a sly off-center grin. "I figured you owed me that much."

"I don't owe you anything!" she snapped.

"Perhaps not," he agreed. He was laughing at her, had been from the moment she stepped into his high-priced office. Like an unsuspecting fly, she'd carelessly gotten caught in a spider's web.

"Stay out of my life," she warned, eyes narrowed.

Evan glared back at her. "Gladly."

Just then Sally, one of Mary Jo's favorite nieces, came skipping down the hallway as only a five-year-old can, completely unaware of the tension between her and Evan. Sally stopped when she saw Mary Jo with Evan.

"Hi," she said, looking up at them.

"Hello, sweetheart," Mary Jo said, forcing herself to smile. Her mouth felt as if it would crack.

Sally stared at Evan, her eyes wide with curiosity. "Are you going to be my uncle someday?"

"No," Mary Jo answered immediately, mortified. It seemed that even her own family had turned against her. "Why not?" Sally wanted to know. "I like him better than Gary, and he likes you, too. I can tell. When we were eating dinner, he kept looking at you. Like Daddy looks at Mommy sometimes."

"I'm dating Gary," Mary Jo insisted, "and he's taking me to a movie. You can come if you want."

Sally shook her head. "Gary likes you, but he doesn't like kids very much."

Mary Jo's heart sank as though it were weighted down with cement blocks. She'd noticed that about Gary herself. He wasn't accustomed to small children; they made him uncomfortable. Kid noise irritated him. Evan, on the other hand, was an instant hit with both the adults and the kids. Nothing her nieces or nephews said or did seemed to bother him. If anything, he appeared to enjoy himself. He'd played volleyball and baseball with her brothers, chess with her father, and wrestled with the kids—ten against one.

"I hope you marry Evan," Sally said, her expression serious. Having stated her opinion, she skipped on down to the end of the hallway.

"Mary Jo."

Before she could say anything else to Evan—although she didn't know what—Gary came looking for her. He stopped abruptly when he saw who she was with.

"I didn't mean to interrupt anything," he said, burying his hands in his pockets, obviously uncomfortable.

"You didn't," Mary Jo answered decisively. "Now, what movie do you think we should see?" She turned her back on Evan and walked toward Gary, knowing in her heart that Sally was right. Evan was the man for her. Not Gary.

"I'M ABSOLUTELY delighted you came," Jessica Dryden said, opening the front door. Mary Jo stepped into the Dryden home, mildly surprised that a maid or other household help hadn't greeted her. From what she remembered of the older Drydens' home, Whispering Willows, the domestic staff had been with them for nearly thirty years.

"Thank you for inviting me," Mary Jo said, looking around. The house was a sprawling rambler decorated with comfortable modern furniture. An ocean scene graced the wall above the fireplace, but it wasn't by an artist Mary Jo recognized. Judging by the decor and relaxed atmosphere, Damian and Jessica seemed to be a fairly typical young couple.

"I fixed us a seafood salad," Jessica said, leading Mary Jo into the large, spotless kitchen. She followed, her eyes taking in everything around her. Jessica and Damian's home was spacious and attractive, but it was nothing like Whispering Willows.

"You made the salad yourself?" Mary Jo asked. She didn't mean to sound rude, but she'd assumed Jessica had kitchen help.

"Yes," Jessica answered pleasantly. "I'm a fairly good cook. At least Damian hasn't complained. Much," she added with a dainty laugh. "I thought we'd eat on the patio. That is, if you don't mind. It's such a beautiful afternoon. I was working in the garden earlier and I cut us some roses. They're so lovely this time of year."

Sliding glass doors led to a brick-lined patio. A round glass table, shaded by a brightly striped umbrella, was set with two pink placemats and linen napkins. A bouquet of yellow roses rested in the middle.

"Would you like iced tea with lunch?" Jessica asked next.

"Please."

"Sit down and I'll bring everything out."

"Let me help." Mary Jo wasn't accustomed to being waited on and would have been uncomfortable letting Jessica do all the work. She followed her new friend into the kitchen and carried out the pitcher of tea while Jessica brought the seafood salad.

"Where's Andy?" Mary Jo asked.

"Napping." She set the salad bowl and matching plates on the table and glanced at her watch. "We'll have a solid hour of peace. I hope."

They sat down together. Jessica gazed at her earnestly and began to speak. "I realize you must think I'm terribly presumptuous to have written you that note, but I'm dying to talk to you."

"I'll admit curiosity is what brought me here," Mary Jo confessed. She'd expected to feel awkward and out of place, but Jessica was so easygoing and unpretentious Mary Jo felt perfectly at ease.

"I've known Evan from the time I was a kid. We grew up next door to each other," Jessica explained. "When I was a teenager I had the biggest crush on him. I made an absolute fool of myself." She shook her head wryly.

Mary Jo thought it was no wonder she found herself liking Jessica so much. They obviously had a great deal in common—especially when it came to Evan!

"As you may be aware, I worked with Evan when he represented Earl Kress. Naturally we spent a good deal of time together. Evan and I became good friends and he told me about you."

Mary Jo nervously smoothed the linen napkin across her lap. She wasn't sure she wanted to hear what Jessica had to say.

"I hurt him deeply, didn't I?" she asked, keeping her head lowered.

"Yes." Apparently Jessica didn't believe in mincing words. "I don't know what happened between you and the man you left Evan for, but clearly it didn't work out the way you expected."

"Few things in life happen the way we expect them to, do they?" Mary Jo answered cryptically.

"No." Jessica set down her fork. "For a while I was convinced there wasn't any hope for Damian and me. You see, I loved Damian, but everyone kept insisting Evan and I should be a couple. It gets confusing, so I won't go into the details, but Damian seemed to think he was doing the noble thing by stepping aside so I could marry Evan. It didn't seem to matter that I was in love with him. Everything was complicated even more by family expectations. Oh, my heavens," she said with a heartfelt sigh, "those were bleak days."

"But you worked everything out."

"Yes," Jessica said with a relaxed smile. "It wasn't easy, but it was sure worth the effort." She paused, resting her hands in her lap. "This is the reason I asked you to have lunch with me. I realize that what happens between you and Evan is none of my business. And knowing Evan, he'd be furious with me if he realized I was even speaking to you, but..." She stopped and took in a deep breath. "You once shared something very special with Evan. I'm hoping that with a little effort on both your parts you can reclaim it."

A cloak of sadness seemed to settle over Mary Jo's shoulders, and when she spoke her words were little more than a whisper. "It isn't possible anymore."

"Why isn't it? I don't know why you've come to Evan. That's none of my affair. But I do realize how much courage it must have taken. You're already halfway there, Mary Jo. Don't give up now."

Mary Jo wished she could believe that, but it was too late for her and Evan now. Whatever chance they'd had as a couple had been destroyed long ago.

By her own hand.

Her reasons for breaking off the relationship hadn't changed. She'd done it because she had to, and she'd done it in such a way that Evan would never forgive her. That was part of her plan—for his own sake.

"In some ways I think Evan hates me," she murmured. Speaking was almost painful; there was a catch in her voice.

"Nonsense," Jessica insisted. "I don't believe that for a moment."

Mary Jo wished she could accept her friend's words, but Jessica hadn't been there when Evan suggested she hire another attorney. She hadn't seen the look in Evan's eyes when she'd confronted him in the hallway of her family home. Nor had she been there when Mary Jo had introduced him to Gary.

He despised her, and the ironic thing was she couldn't blame him.

"Just remember what I said," Jessica urged. "Be patient with Evan, and with yourself. But most of all, don't give up, not until you're convinced it'll never work. I speak from experience, Mary Jo—the rewards are well worth whatever it costs your pride. I can't imagine my life without Damian and Andy."

After a brief silence, Mary Jo resolutely changed the subject, and the two women settled down to their meal. Conversation was lighthearted—books and movies they'd both enjoyed, anecdotes about friends and family, opinions about various public figures.

They were continuing a good-natured disagreement over one of the Red Sox pitchers as they carried their plates back inside. Just as they reached the kitchen, the doorbell chimed.

"I'll get that," Jessica said.

Smiling, Mary Jo rinsed off the plates and placed them in the dishwasher. She liked Jessica very much. Damian's wife was open and natural and had a wonderful sense of humor. She was also deeply in love with her husband.

"It's Evan," Jessica said, returning to the kitchen. Her voice was strained and tense. Evan stood stiffly behind his sister-in-law. "He dropped off some papers for Damian."

"Uh, hello, Evan," Mary Jo said awkwardly.

Jessica's gaze pleaded with her to believe she hadn't arranged this accidental meeting.

Andy let out a piercing cry, and Mary Jo decided the toddler had the worst sense of timing of any baby she'd ever known.

Jessica excused herself, and Mary Jo was left standing next to the dishwasher, wishing she were anyplace else in the world.

"What are you doing here?" he demanded the minute Jessica was out of earshot.

"You showed up at *my* family's home. Why is it so shocking that I'm at your brother's house?"

"I was invited," he reminded her fiercely.

"So was I."

He looked for a moment as if he didn't believe her. "Fine. I suppose you and Jessica have decided to become bosom buddies. That sounds like something you'd do."

Mary Jo didn't have a response to such a patently unfair remark.

"As it happens," Evan said in a clear effort to put his anger behind him, "I was meaning to call you this afternoon, anyway."

"About my parents' case?" she asked anxiously.

"I've talked with my colleague about Adison Investments, and it looks as if it'll involve some lengthy litigation."

Mary Jo leaned against the kitchen counter. "Lengthy is another word for expensive, right?"

"I was prepared to discuss my fee with you at the same time," he continued in a businesslike tone.

"All right," she said, tensing.

"I can't see this costing anything less than six or seven thousand."

She couldn't help a sharp intake of breath. That amount of money was a fortune to her parents. To her, too.

"It could go even higher."

Which was another way of saying he wasn't willing to handle the case. Mary Jo felt the sudden need to sit down. She walked over to the table, pulled out a chair and plunked herself down.

"I'd be willing to do what I can, but—"

"Don't lie to me, Evan," she said, fighting back her hurt and frustration. She'd come to him because he had the clout and the influence to help her family. Because he was a damn good attorney. Because she'd trusted him to be honest and ethical.

"I'm not lying."

"Six or seven thousand dollars is far beyond what my parents or I can afford. That may not be a lot of money to you or your family, but there's no way we could hope to raise that much in a short amount of time."

"I'm willing to take payments."

How very generous of him, she mused sarcastically.

"There might be another way," he said.

"What?"

"If you agree, of course."

Mary Jo wasn't sure she liked the sound of this.

"A summer job. You're out of school, aren't you?"

She nodded.

"My secretary, Mrs. Sterling, is taking an extended European vacation this summer. I'd intended to hire a replacement, but as I recall your typing and dictation skills are excellent."

"My typing skills are minimal and I never took shorthand."

He grinned as if that didn't matter. Obviously, what did matter was making her miserable for the next two months.

"But you're a fast learner. Am I right or wrong?" he pressed.

"Well . . . I do pick up things up fairly easily."

"That's what I thought." He spread out his hands. "Now, do you want the job or not?"

CHAPTER FOUR

"MR. DRYDEN's a real pleasure to work for. I'm sure you won't have any problems," Mrs. Sterling said, looking absolutely delighted that Mary Jo would be substituting for her. "Evan's not the least bit demanding, and I can't think of even one time when he's been unreasonable."

Mary Jo suspected that might not be the case with her.

"I could have retired with my husband, but I enjoy my job so much I decided to stay on," Mrs. Sterling continued. "I couldn't bear leaving that young man. In some ways, I think of Evan as my own son."

"I'm sure he reciprocates your feelings," Mary Jo said politely. She didn't know how much longer she could endure listening to this list of Evan's finer qualities. Not that she doubted they were true. For Mrs. Sterling.

Thus far, Evan had embarrassed her in front of her family and blackmailed her into working for him. She had a problem picturing him as Prince Charming to her Cinderella. As for his being a "real pleasure" to work for, Mary Jo entertained some serious reservations.

"I'm glad you've got the opportunity to travel with your husband," Mary Jo added.

"That's another thing," Evan's secretary gushed. "What boss would be willing to let his secretary go for two whole months like this? It's a terrible inconvenience to him. Nevertheless, Mr. Dryden encouraged me to take this trip with Dennis. Why, he *insisted* I go. I promise you, they don't come any better than Mr. Dryden. You're going to thoroughly enjoy your summer."

Mary Jo's smile was weak at best.

Evan wanted her under his thumb, and much as she disliked giving in to the pressure, she had no choice. Six or seven thousand dollars would financially cripple her parents. Evan knew that. He was also well aware that her brothers weren't in any position to help.

With the slump in the economy, new construction starts had been way down. Jack, Rich and Lonny had collected unemployment benefits most of the winter and were just scraping by now. Bill and Mark's automotive business was barely on its feet.

She was the one who'd gone to Evan for help, and she was the one who'd accepted the financial responsibility. When she'd told her parents she'd be working for Evan, they were both delighted. Her mother seemed to think it was the perfect solution. Whether Evan had planned it this way or not, his employing her had helped smooth her father's ruffled feathers about Evan's fee. Apparently, letting her pick up any out-of-pocket expenses was unacceptable to Norman Summerhill, but an exchange of services, so to speak, was fine.

Evan, who could do no wrong as far as her parents were concerned, came out of this smelling like a rose, to use one of her dad's favorite expressions.

Mary Jo wondered if she was being unfair to assume that Evan was looking for vengeance, for a means of making her life miserable. Perhaps she'd misjudged him.

Perhaps. But she sincerely doubted it.

"I'm taking my lunch now," Mrs. Sterling said, pulling open the bottom drawer of her desk and taking out her handbag. She hesitated. "You will be all right here by yourself, won't you?"

"Of course." Mary Jo made an effort to sound infinitely confident, even if she wasn't. Evan's legal assistant, Peter McNichols, was on vacation for the next couple of weeks, so she'd be dealing with Evan entirely on her own.

Mary Jo wasn't sure she was emotionally prepared for that just yet. The shaky, unsure feeling in the pit of her stomach reminded her of the first time she'd stood in front of a classroom filled with five-year-olds.

No sooner had Mrs. Sterling left when Evan summoned Mary Jo. Grabbing a pen and pad, she hurried into his office, determined to be the best substitute secretary he could have hired.

"Sit down," he instructed in a brisk, businesslike tone.

Mary Jo complied, sitting on the very edge of the chair, her back ramrod-straight, her shoulders stiff.

He reached for a small, well-worn black book and flipped through the flimsy pages, scrutinizing the names. Mary Jo realized it had to be the typical bachelor's infamous "black book." She knew he had a reputation, after all, as one of Boston's most eligible bachelors. Every six months or so, gossip columns speculated on Evan Dryden's current love interest. A little black book was exactly what she expected of him.

"Order a dozen red roses to be sent to Catherine Moore," he said, and rattled off the address. Mary Jo immediately recognized it as being in a prestigious neighborhood. "Suggest we meet for lunch on the twenty-fifth. Around twelve-thirty." He mentioned one of Boston's most elegant restaurants. "Have you got that?" he asked.

"I'll see to it immediately," Mary Jo said crisply, revealing none of her feelings. Evan had done this on purpose. He was having her arrange a lunch date with one of his many conquests in order to humiliate her, to teach her a lesson. It was his way of telling her that he'd recovered completely from their short-lived romance. There were any number of women who would welcome his attentions.

Well, Mary Jo got the message, loud and clear. She stood, ready to return to her desk.

"There's more," Evan said.

Mary Jo sat back down and was barely able to keep up with him as he listed name after name, followed by phone number and address. Each woman was to receive a dozen red roses and an invitation to lunch, with time and place suggested.

When he'd finished, Mary Jo counted six names, each conjuring up a statuesque beauty. No doubt every one of them could run circles around her in looks, talent and, most important, social position.

Mary Jo didn't realize one man could find that many places to eat with so many different women, but she wisely kept her opinion to herself. If he was hoping she'd give him the satisfaction of a response, he was dead wrong.

She'd just finished ordering the flowers when Damian Dryden stepped into the office.

"Hello," he said. His eyes widened with surprise at finding her sitting at Mrs. Sterling's desk.

Mary Jo stood and extended her hand. "I'm Mary Jo Summerhill. We met briefly last week." She didn't mention the one other time she'd been introduced to Damian, certain he wouldn't remember.

It was well over three years ago. Evan and Mary Jo had been sailing, and they'd run into Damian at the marina. Her first impression of Evan's older brother was that of a shrewd businessman. Damian had seemed stiff and somewhat distant. He'd shown little interest in their cheerful commentary on sailing and the weather. From conversations she'd previously had with Evan regarding his brother, she'd learned he was a serious and hardworking lawyer, and that was certainly how he'd struck her—as someone with no time for fun or frivolity. Currently, he was a Superior Court judge, but he often stopped in at the family law firm. Apparently the two brothers were close friends, as well as brothers.

The man she'd met on the dock that day and the one who stood before her now might have been two entirely different men. Damian remained serious and hardworking, but he was more relaxed now, more apt to smile. Mary Jo was convinced that marriage and fatherhood had made the difference, and she was genuinely happy for him and for Jessica. They seemed perfect for each other.

"You're working for the firm now?" Damian asked.

"Mrs. Sterling will be traveling in Europe this summer," Mary Jo explained, "and Evan, uh, offered me the job." Which was a polite way of saying he'd coerced her into accepting the position.

"But I thought—" Damian stopped abruptly, then grinned. "Is Evan in?"

"Yes. I'll tell him you're here." She reached for the intercom switch and announced Damian, who walked directly into Evan's office.

Mary Jo was acquainting herself with the filing system when she heard Evan burst out laughing. It really wasn't fair to assume it had something to do with her, but she couldn't help believing that was the case.

Damian left a couple of minutes later, smiling. He paused in front of Mary Jo's desk. "Don't let him give you a hard time," he said pleasantly. "My wife mentioned having you over for lunch last week, but she didn't say you'd accepted a position with the firm."

"I . . . I didn't know it myself at the time," Mary Jo mumbled. She hadn't actually agreed to the job until much later, after she'd spent a few days sorting through her limited options.

"I see. Well, it's good to have you on board, Mary Jo. If you have any questions or concerns, don't hesitate to talk to Evan. And if he does give you a hard time, just let me know and I'll straighten him out."

"Thank you," she said, and meant it. Although she couldn't very well see herself complaining to one brother about the other. . . .

She decided to change her attitude about the whole situation. She'd forget about Evan's probable motives and, instead, start looking at the positive side of this opportunity. She'd be able to help her parents now, without dipping into her own savings. Things could definitely be worse.

Mary Jo didn't learn just how *much* worse until Wednesday—the first day she was working on her own. Mrs. Sterling had spent the first two days of the week acquainting Mary Jo with office procedures and the filing system. She'd updated her on Evan's current cases, and Mary Jo felt reasonably confident she could handle whatever came up.

He called her into his office around eleven. "I need the William Jenkins file."

"I'll have it for you right away," she assured him. Mary Jo returned to the outer office and the filing cabinet, and sorted through the colored tabs. She located three clients named Jenkins, none of whom was William. Her heart started to pound with dread as she hurried to another filing drawer, thinking it might have been misfiled.

Five minutes passed. Evan came out of his office, his movements as brusque and irritated as his voice. "Is there a problem?"

"I . . . can't seem to find the William Jenkins file," she said, hurriedly riffling through the files one more time. "Are you sure it isn't on your desk?"

"Would I have asked you to find it if I had it on my desk?" She could feel his cold stare directly between the shoulder blades.

"No, I guess not. But it isn't out here."

"It has to be. I distinctly remember giving it to Mrs. Sterling on Monday."

"She had me replace all the files on Monday," Mary Jo admitted reluctantly.

"Then you must have misfiled it."

"I don't recall any file with the name Jenkins," she said stubbornly. She didn't want to make an issue of this, but she'd been extremely careful with every file, even double-checking her work.

"Are you telling me I *didn't* return the file? Are you calling me a liar?"

This wasn't going well. "No," she said in a slow, deliberate voice. "All I'm saying is that I don't recall replacing any file with the name Jenkins on it." Their gazes met and locked in silent battle.

Evan's dark eyes narrowed briefly. "Are you doing this on purpose, Mary Jo?" he asked, crossing his arms over his chest.

"Absolutely not." Outraged, she brought her chin up and met his glare. "You can think whatever you like of me, but I'd never do anything so underhanded as hide an important file."

She wasn't sure if he believed her or not, and his lack of trust hurt her more than any words he might have spoken. "If you honestly suspect I'd sabotage your office, then I suggest you fire me immediately."

Evan walked over to the cabinet and pulled open the top drawer. He was searching through the files, the same way she had earlier.

Silently Mary Jo prayed she hadn't inadvertently missed seeing the requested file. The humiliation of having him find it would be unbearable.

"It isn't here," he murmured, sounding almost surprised.

Mary Jo gave an inward sigh of relief.

"Where could it possibly be?" he asked impatiently. "I need it for an appointment this afteroon."

Mary Jo edged a couple of steps toward him. "Would you mind if I looked in your office?"

He gestured toward the open door. "By all means."

She sorted through the stack of files on the corner of his desk and leafed through his briefcase, all to no avail. Glancing at the clock, she groaned inwardly. "You have a luncheon appointment," she reminded him.

"I need that file!" he snapped.

Mary Jo bristled. "I'm doing my best."

"Your best clearly isn't good enough. *Find that file.*"

"I'll do a much better job of it if you aren't here breathing down my neck. Go and have lunch, and I'll find the Jenkins file." She'd dismantle the filing cabinets one by one until she'd located it, if that was what it took.

Evan hesitated, then glanced at his watch. "I won't be long," he muttered, reaching for his jacket and thrusting his arms into the sleeves. "I'll give you a call from the restaurant."

"All right."

"If worse comes to worst, we can reschedule the client," he said as he buttoned the jacket. Evan had always been a smart dresser, she reflected irrelevantly. No matter what the circumstances, he looked as if he'd just stepped off a page in *Esquire* or *G.Q.*

"Look" Evan said, pausing at the door. "Don't worry about it. The file has to surface sometime." He seemed to be apologizing, however indirectly, for his earlier bout of bad temper.

She nodded, feeling guilty although she had no reason. But the file was missing and she felt responsible, despite the fact that she'd never so much as seen it.

Since she'd brought her lunch with her to work, Mary Jo nibbled at it as she sorted through every single file drawer in every single cabinet. Mrs. Sterling was meticulously neat, and not a single file had been misplaced.

Mary Jo was sitting on the carpet, files spread around her, when Evan phoned.

"Did you find it?"

"No, I'm sorry, Evan... Mr. Dryden," she corrected quickly.

His lengthy pause added to her feelings of guilt and confusion. She'd been so determined to be a good replacement. By heaven, she'd vowed, she was going to give him his money's worth. Yet here it was—her day of working alone—and already she'd failed him.

By the time Evan was back at the office, she'd reassembled everything. He made the call to reschedule the appointment with William Jenkins, saving her the task of inventing an excuse.

At three o'clock her phone rang. It was Gary, and the instant she recognized his voice, Mary Jo groaned inwardly.

"How'd you know where to reach me?" she asked, keeping her voice low. Evan was sure to frown on personal phone calls, especially from a male friend. After their confrontation that morning, she felt bad enough.

"Your mom told me you were working for Daddy Warbucks now."

"Don't call him that," she said heatedly, surprised at the flash of anger she experienced.

Gary was silent, as if he, too, was taken back by her outburst. "I apologize," he said, sounding genuinely contrite. "I didn't phone to start an argument. I wanted you to know I've taken our talk last Sunday to heart. How about dinner and dancing this Saturday? We could go to one of those all-you-can-eat places that serve barbecued ribs, and shuffle our feet a little afterward."

"Uh, maybe we could talk about this later."

"Yes or no?" Gary cajoled. "Just how difficult can it be? I thought you'd be pleased."

"It isn't a good idea to call me at the office, Gary."

"But I'll be at the fire station by the time you're off work," he explained. "I thought you wanted us to spend more time together. That's what you said, isn't it?"

Was that what she'd said? She didn't think so. Not exactly. "Uh, well . . ." Why, oh why, was life so complicated?

"I'm glad you spoke up," Gary continued when she didn't, "because I tend to get lazy in a relationship. I want you to know how much I appreciate your company."

"All right, I'll go," she said ungraciously, knowing it was the only way she was likely to get him off the phone quickly. "Saturday evening. What time?"

"Six okay?. I'll pick you up."

"Six is fine."

"We're going to have a great time, Mary Jo. Just you wait and see."

She wasn't at all convinced of that, but she supposed she didn't have any right to complain. Eager to please, Gary was doing exactly what she'd asked of him. And frankly, dinner with Gary was a damn sight better than sitting home alone.

No sooner had she hung up the phone when Evan opened his door and stared at her, his look hard and disapproving. He didn't say a word about personal phone calls. He didn't have to. The heat radiated from her cheeks.

"Th-that was Gary," she said, then wanted to kick herself for volunteering the information. "I explained that I can't take personal phone calls at the office. He won't be phoning again."

"Good," he said, and closed the door. It clicked sharply into place, as if to underline his disapproval. She returned to the letter she was typing into the computer.

Just before five, Mary Jo collected the letters that required Evan's signature and carried them to his office. He was reading over a brief, and momentarily glanced up when she knocked softly and entered the room.

"Is there anything else you'd like me to do before I leave?" she asked, depositing the unsigned letters onto the corner of his desk.

He shook his head. "Nothing, thank you. Good night, Ms. Summerhill."

He sounded so stiff and formal. As if he'd never held her, never kissed her. As if she'd never meant anything to him and never would.

"Good night, Mr. Dryden." She turned quickly and walked out of the office.

After their brief exchange regarding the missing file, they'd been coolly polite to each other during the rest of the day.

If his intention was to punish her, he couldn't have devised a more effective means.

Because she loved Evan. She'd never stopped loving him, no matter how she tried to convince herself otherwise. Being with him every day and maintaining this crisp, professional facade was the cruelest form of punishment.

Once she was home, Mary Jo kicked off her low heels, slumped into the rocking chair and closed her eyes in a desperate attempt to relax. She hadn't worked for Evan a full week yet, and already she wondered if she could last another day.

The rest of the summer didn't bear thinking about.

"WHAT I DON'T UNDERSTAND," Marianna Summerhill said as she chopped up chicken for the summer salad, "is why you and Evan ever broke up."

"Mom, please, it was a long time ago."

"Not so long. Two, three years."

"Do you want me to set the table?" Mary Jo asked, hoping to distract her mother. That she hadn't seen through this unexpected dinner invitation only showed how weary she was, how low her defenses. Her mother had phoned only the evening before, when Mary Jo was still recovering from working on her own with Evan; she'd insisted Mary Jo join them for dinner and "a nice visit."

"So, how's the job going?" her father asked, sitting down at the kitchen table. The huge dining room table was reserved for Sunday dinners with as many of the family that could come.

"Oh, just great," Mary Jo said, working up enough energy to offer him a reassuring smile. She didn't want her parents to know what the job was costing her emotionally.

"I was just saying to Mary Jo what a fine young man Evan Dryden is." Her mother set the salad in the center of the table and pulled out a chair.

"He certainly is a decent sort. You were dating him a while back, weren't you?"

"Yes, Dad."

"Seems to me the two of you were real serious." When she didn't immediately answer, he added, "As I recall, he gave you an engagement ring, didn't he? You had him come to dinner that one time. Whatever happened, Mary Jo? Did our family scare him off?"

Mary Jo was forever bound to hide the truth. Evan had been an instant hit with her family. They'd thrown open their arms and welcomed him, delighted that Mary Jo had found a man to love. Not for the world would she let her parents be hurt. Not for the world would she tell them the truth.

How could she possibly explain that their only daughter, whom they adored, wasn't good enough for the high-and-mighty Drydens? The minute Mary Jo met Evan's mother, she sensed the older woman's disappointment in her. Lois Dryden was looking for more in a daughter-in-law than Mary Jo could ever be.

Their private chat after dinner had set the record straight. Evan was destined for politics and would need a certain type of wife, Mrs. Dryden had gently explained. Mary Jo didn't hear much beyond that.

Mrs. Dryden had strongly implied that Mary Jo would hinder Evan's political aspirations. She might very well ruin his life. There'd been some talk about destiny and family expectations and the demands on a political wife—Mary Jo's memories of the conversation were vague. But her understanding of Mrs. Dryden's message had been anything but.

Evan needed a woman who would be an asset—socially and politically. As an electrician's daughter, Mary Jo couldn't possibly be that woman. End of discussion.

"Mary Jo?"

Her mother's worried voice cut into her thoughts. She shook her head and smiled. "I'm sorry, Mom, what were you saying?"

"Your father asked you a question."

"About you and Evan," Norman elaborated. "I thought you two were pretty serious."

"We were serious at one time," she admitted, seeing no other way around it. "We were even engaged. But we...drifted apart. Those things happen, you know. Luckily we realized that before it was too late."

"But he's such a dear boy."

"He's a charmer, Mom," Mary Jo said, making light of his appeal. "But he's not the man for me. Besides, I'm dating Gary now."

Her parents exchanged meaningful glances.

"You don't like Gary?" Mary Jo prodded.

"Of course we like him," Marianna said cautiously. "It's just that...well, he's very sweet, but frankly, Mary Jo, I just don't see Gary as the man for you."

Frankly, Mary Jo didn't, either.

"It seems to me," her father said slowly while he buttered a slice of bread, "that your young man's more interested in your mother's cooking than he is in you."

So the family had noticed. Not that Gary'd made any secret of it. "Gary's just a friend, Dad. You don't need to worry—we aren't really serious."

"What about Evan?" Marianna studied Mary Jo carefully, wearing the concerned expression she always wore whenever she suspected one of her children was ill. An intense, narrowed expression—as if staring at Mary Jo long enough would reveal the problem.

"Oh, Evan's a friend, too," Mary Jo said airily, but she didn't really believe it. She doubted they could ever be friends again.

LATE FRIDAY AFTERNOON, just before she began getting ready to leave for the weekend, Evan called Mary Jo into his office. He was busy writing, and she waited until he'd finished before she asked, "You wanted to see me?"

"Yes," he said absently, reaching for a file folder. "I'm afraid I'm going to need you tomorrow."

"On Saturday?" She'd assumed the weekends were her own.

"I'm sure Mrs. Sterling mentioned I might occasionally need you to travel with me."

"No, she didn't," Mary Jo said, holding her shoulders rigid. She could guess what was coming. Somehow he was going to keep her from seeing Gary Saturday night. A man who lunched with a different woman every day of the week wanted to cheat her out of one dinner date with a friend.

"As it happens, I'll need you tomorrow afternoon and evening. I'm driving up to—"

"As it happens I already have plans for tomorrow evening," she interrupted defiantly.

"Then I suggest you cancel," he said impassively. "According to the terms of our agreement, you're to be at my disposal for the next two months. I need you this Saturday afternoon and evening."

"Yes, but—"

"May I remind you, that you're being well compensated for your time?"

It would take more than counting to ten to cool Mary Jo's rising temper. She wasn't fooled. Not for a second. Evan was doing this on purpose. He'd overheard her conversation with Gary.

"And if I refuse?" she asked, her outrage and defiance evident in every syllable.

Evan shrugged, as if it wasn't his concern one way or the other. "Then I'll have no choice but to fire you."

The temptation to throw the job back in his face was so strong she had to close her eyes to control it. "You're doing this intentionally, aren't you?" she asked between gritted teeth. "I have a date with Gary Saturday night—you know I do—and you want to ruin it."

Evan leaned forward in his black leather chair; he seemed to weigh his words carefully. "Despite what you might think, I'm not a vindictive man. But, Ms. Summerhill, it doesn't really matter *what* you think."

She bit down so hard, her teeth hurt. "You're right, of course," she said quietly. "It doesn't matter what I think." She whirled around and stalked out of his office.

The force of her anger was too great to let her sit still. For ten minutes, she paced the office floor, then slumped into her chair. Resting her elbows on the desk, she buried her face in her hands, feeling very close to tears. It wasn't that this date with Gary was so important. It was that Evan would purposely ruin it for her.

"Mary Jo."

She dropped her hands to find Evan standing in front of her desk. They stared at one another for a long, still moment, then Mary Jo looked away. She wanted to wipe out the past and find the man she'd once loved. But she knew that what *he* wanted was to hurt her, to pay her back for the pain she'd caused him.

"What time do you need me?" she asked in an expressionless voice. She refused to meet his gaze.

"Three-thirty. I'll pick you up at your place."

"I'll be ready."

In the ensuing silence, Damian walked casually into the room. He stopped when he noticed them, glancing from Evan to Mary Jo and back again.

"I'm not interrupting anything, am I?"

"No." Evan recovered first and was quick to reassure his older brother. "What can I do for you, Damian?"

Damian gestured with the file he carried. "I read over the Jenkins case like you asked and jotted down some notes. I thought you might want to go over them with me."

The name Jenkins leapt out at Mary Jo. "Did you say *Jenkins?*" she asked excitedly.

"Why, yes. Evan gave me the file the other day and asked me for my opinion."

"I did?" Evan sounded genuinely shocked.

Damian frowned. "Don't you remember?"

"No," Evan said, "Good Lord, Mary Jo and I've been searching for that file since yesterday."

"All you had to do, little brother," Damian chided, "was ask me."

The two men disappeared into Evan's office while Mary Jo finished tidying up for the day. Damian left as she was gathering up her personal things.

"Evan would like to see you for a moment," he said on his way out the door.

Setting her purse aside, she walked into Evan's office. "You wanted to see me?" she asked coldly, standing just inside the doorway.

He stood at the window, staring down at the street far below, his hands clasped behind his back. His shoulders were slumped as if he'd grown weary. He turned to face her, his expression composed, even cool. "I apologize for the screw-up over the Jenkins file. I was entirely at fault. I did give it to Damian to read. I'm afraid it completely slipped my mind."

His apology came as a surprise. "It's no problem," she murmured.

"About tomorrow," he said next, his voice dropping slightly, "I won't be needing you, after all. Enjoy your evening with lover boy."

CHAPTER FIVE

"Is EVAN COMING?" Mary Jo's oldest brother, Jack, asked as he passed the bowl of mashed potatoes to his wife, Cathy.

"Yeah," Lonny piped in. "Where's Evan?"

"I heard you were working for him now," Cathy said, adding under her breath, "Lucky you."

Mary Jo's family was sitting around the big dining room table. Jack, Cathy and their three children, Lonny and his wife, Sandra, and their two kids, plus her parents—they'd all focused their attention on Mary Jo.

"Mr. Dryden doesn't tell me his plans," she said stiffly, uncomfortable with their questions.

"You call him 'Mr. Dryden?'" her father quizzed, frowning.

"I'm his employee," Mary Jo replied.

"His father is a senator," Marianna reminded her husband, as if this was important information he didn't already know.

"I thought you said Evan's your friend." Her father wasn't going to give up, Mary Jo realized, until he had the answers he wanted.

"He *is* my friend," she returned evenly, "but while I'm an employee of the law firm it's important to maintain a certain decorum." That was a good response, she thought a bit smugly. One her father couldn't dispute.

"Did you invite him to Sunday dinner, dear?" her mother wanted to know.

"No."

"Then that explains it," Marianna said with a disappointed sigh. "Next week I'll see to it myself. We owe him a big debt of thanks."

Mary Jo resisted telling her mother that a man like Evan Dryden had more important things to do than plan his Sunday afternoons around her family's dinner. He'd come once as a gesture of friendliness, but they shouldn't expect him again. Her mother would learn that soon enough.

"How's the case with Adison Investments going, M.J.?" Jack asked, stabbing his fork into a marinated vegetable. "Have you heard anything?"

"Not yet," Mary Jo answered. "Evan had Mrs. Sterling type up a letter last week. I believe she mailed Mom and Dad a copy."

"She did," her father inserted.

"From my understanding, Evan, er, Mr. Dryden, gave Adison Investments two weeks to respond. If he hasn't heard from them by then, he'll prepare a lawsuit."

"Does he expect them to answer?" Rich burst out, his dark eyes flashing with anger.

"Now, son, don't get all riled up over this. Evan and Mary Jo are handling it now, and I have complete faith that justice will be served."

The family returned their attention to their food, and when the conversation moved on to other subjects, Mary Jo was grateful. Then, out of the blue, when she least expected it, her mother asked, "How'd your dinner date go with Gary?"

Taken aback, she stopped chewing, the fork poised in front of her mouth. Why was her life of such interest all of a sudden?

"Fine," she murmured when she'd swallowed. Once again the family's attention was on her. "Why is everyone looking at me?" she demanded.

Lonny chuckled. "It might be that we're wondering why you'd date someone like Gary Copeland when you could be going out with Evan Dryden."

"I doubt very much that Evan dates his employees," she said righteously. "It's bad business practice."

"I like Evan a whole lot," five-year-old Sally piped in. "You do, too, don't you, Aunt Mary Jo?"

"Hmm...yes," she admitted, knowing she'd never get away with a lie, at least not with her own family. They knew her too well.

"Where's Gary now?" her oldest brother asked as though he'd only just noticed that her date hadn't joined them for dinner. "It seems to me he's generally here. You'd think the guy had never tasted home cooking."

Now was as good a time as any to explain, Mary Jo decided. "Gary and I decided not to see each other anymore, Jack," she said, hoping to gloss over the details. "We're both doing different things now, and we've...drifted apart."

"Isn't that what you were telling me about you and Evan Dryden?" her father asked thoughtfully.

Mary Jo had forgotten that. Indeed, it was exactly what she'd said.

"Seems to me," her father added with a knowing parental look, "that you've been doing a lot of drifting apart from people lately."

Her mother, bless her heart, cast Mary Jo's father a frown. "If you ask me, it's the other way around." She nodded once as if to say the subject was now closed.

In some ways, Mary Jo was going to miss Gary. He was a friend and they'd parted on friendly terms. She hadn't intended to end their relationship, but over dinner Gary had suggested they think seriously about their future together.

To put it mildly, she'd been shocked. She'd felt comfortable in their rather loose relationship. Now Gary was looking for something more. She wasn't.

She realized he'd been disappointed, but he'd seemed to accept and appreciate her honesty.

"I like Evan better, anyway," Sally said solemnly. She nodded once like her grandmother had just done, and the pink ribbons on her pigtails bobbed. "You'll bring him to dinner now, won't you?"

"I don't know, sweetheart."

"I do," her mother said, smiling confidently. "A mother knows these things, and it seems to me that Evan Dryden is the perfect man for our Mary Jo."

EVAN WAS IN THE OFFICE when Mary Jo arrived early Monday morning. She quickly prepared a pot of coffee and brought him a mug as soon as it was ready.

He was on the phone but glanced up when she entered his office and smiled his appreciation as he accepted the coffee. She returned to the outer office, amazed—and a little frightened—by how much one of his smiles could affect her.

Mary Jo's greatest fear was that the longer they worked together the more difficult it would be for her to maintain her guard. Without being aware of it, she might reveal her true feelings for Evan.

The phone rang and she automatically reached for it, enjoying her role as Evan's secretary. She and Evan had had their share of differences, but seemed to have resolved them. In the office, anyway.

"Mary Jo." It was Jessica Dryden on the line.

Mary Jo stiffened, fearing Evan might hear her taking a personal call. She didn't want anything to jeopardize their newly amicable relationship. The door to his office was open and he had a clear view of her from his desk.

"May I help you?" she asked in her best secretary voice.

Jessica hesitated at her cool, professional tone. "Hey, it's me. Jessica."

"I realize that."

Jessica laughed lightly. "I get it. Evan must be listening."

"That's correct." Mary Jo had trouble hiding a smile. One chance look in her direction, and he'd know this was no client she had on the line.

"Damian told me you're working for Evan now. What happened?" Jessica's voice lowered to a whisper as if she feared Evan would hear her, too.

Mary Jo carefully weighed her words. "I believe that case involved blackmail."

"Blackmail?" Jessica repeated, and laughed outright. "This I've got to hear. Is he being a real slave driver?"

"No. Not exactly."

"Can you escape one afternoon and meet me for lunch?"

"I might be able to arrange a luncheon appointment. What day would you suggest?"

"How about tomorrow at noon? There's an Italian restaurant around the corner in the basement of the Wellman building. The food's great and the people who own it are like family."

"That sounds acceptable."

Evan appeared in the doorway between his office and hers. He studied her closely. Mary Jo swallowed uncomfortably at the obvious censure in his expression.

"Uh, perhaps I could confirm the details with you later."

Jessica laughed again. "Judging by your voice, Evan's standing right there—and he's figured out this isn't a business call."

"I believe you're right," she said stiffly.

Jessica seemed absolutely delighted. "I can't wait to hear all about this. I'll see you tomorrow, and Mary Jo..."

"Yes?" she urged, eager to get off the line.

"Have you thought any more about what I said? About working things out with Evan?"

"I . . . I'm thinking."

"Good. That's just great. I'll see you tomorrow, then."

Mary Jo replaced the receiver and darted a look in Evan's direction. He averted his eyes and slammed the door shut. As if he was furious with her. Worse, as if she disgusted him.

Stunned, Mary Jo sat at her desk, fighting back a surge of outrage. He was being unfair. At the very least, he could have given her the opportunity to explain!

The morning, which had started out so well, with a smile and a sense of promise, had quickly disintegrated into outright hostility. Evan ignored her for the rest of the morning, not speaking except about office matters. And even then, his voice was cold and impatient. The brusque, hurried instructions, the lack of eye contact—everything seemed to suggest he could barely tolerate the sight of her.

Without a word of farewell, he left at noon for his luncheon engagement and returned promptly at one-thirty, a scant few minutes before his first afternoon appointment. Mary Jo had begun to wonder if he planned to return at all, worrying about how she'd explain his absence if anyone called.

The temperature seemed to drop perceptibly the moment Evan walked in the door. She tensed, debating whether or not to confront him about his attitude.

Evan had changed, Mary Jo mused defeatedly. She couldn't remember him ever being this temperamental. She felt as though she were walking on the proverbial eggshells, afraid of saying or doing something that would irritate him even more.

Her afternoon was miserable. By five o'clock she knew she couldn't take much more of this silent treatment. She waited until the switchboard had been turned over to the answering service; that way there was no risk of being interrupted by a phone call.

The office was quiet—presumably almost everyone

else had gone home—when she approached his door. She knocked, then immediately walked inside. He was working and seemed unaware of her presence. She stood there silently until he glanced up.

"Could I speak to you for a moment?" she asked, standing stiffly in front of his desk. She heard the small quaver in her voice and groaned inwardly. She'd wanted to sound strong and confident.

"Is there a problem?" Evan asked, raising his eyebrows as if surprised—and not pleasantly—by her request.

"I'm afraid my position here isn't working out."

"Oh?" Up went the eyebrows again. "And why isn't it?"

It was much too difficult to explain how deeply his moods affected her. A mere smile and she was jubilant, a frown and she was cast into despair.

"It . . . it just isn't," was the best she could do.

"Am I too demanding?"

"No," she admitted reluctantly.

"Unreasonable?"

She lowered her gaze and shook her head.

"Then what is it?" he demanded.

She gritted her teeth. "I want you to know that I've never made a personal phone call from this office during working hours."

"True, but you've received them."

"I assured you Gary wouldn't be phoning me again."

"But he did," Evan inserted smoothly.

"He most certainly did not," she said righteously.

"Mary Jo," he said with exaggerated patience, as though he were speaking to a child, "I heard you arranging a luncheon date with him myself."

"That was Jessica. Damian mentioned running into me at the office and she called and suggested we meet for lunch."

"Jessica," Evan muttered. He grew strangely quiet.

"I think it might be best if I sought employment elsewhere," Mary Jo concluded. "Naturally I'll be happy to train my replacement." She turned abruptly and started to leave.

"Mary Jo." He sighed heavily. "Listen, you're right. I've behaved like a jerk all day. I apologize. Your personal life, your phone calls—it's none of my business. I promise you this won't happen again."

Mary Jo paused, unsure what to think. She certainly hadn't expected an apology.

"I want you to stay on," he added. "You've been doing an excellent job, and I've been unfair. Will you?"

She should refuse, walk out while she had the excuse to do so. Leave without regrets. But she couldn't. She simply couldn't.

She offered him a shaky smile and nodded. "You know, you're not such a curmudgeon to work for, after all."

"I'm not?" He sounded downright cheerful. "This calls for a celebration, don't you think? Do you still enjoy sailing as much as you used to?"

She hadn't been on the water since the last time they'd taken out his sailboat. "I think so," she murmured, head spinning at his sudden reversal.

"Great. Run home and change clothes and meet me at the marina in an hour. We'll take out my boat and discover if you've still got your sea legs."

The prospect of spending time with Evan was too wonderful to turn down. For her sanity's sake, she should think twice before accepting the invitation, but she didn't. Whatever the price, she'd willingly pay it— later.

"Remember when I taught you to sail?" Evan asked, his eyes smiling.

Mary Jo couldn't keep herself from smiling back. He'd been infinitely patient with her. She came from a long line of landlubbers and was convinced she'd never become a sailor.

"I still remember the first time we pulled out of the marina with me at the helm. I rammed another sailboat," she reminded him, and they both laughed.

"You'll meet me?" Evan asked, oddly intense after their moment of lightness.

Mary Jo doubted she could have refused him anything. "Just don't ask me to motor the boat out of the slip."

"You've got yourself a deal."

A few hours earlier, she'd believed she couldn't last another hour working with Evan. Now here she was, agreeing to meet him after hours for a sailing lesson.

Rushing home, she threw off her clothes, not bothering to hang them up the way she usually did. She didn't stay longer than the few minutes it took to pull on a pair of jeans, a sweatshirt and her deck shoes. Any time for reflection, and Mary Jo was afraid she'd talk herself out of going. She wanted these few hours with Evan so much it hurt.

Right now she refused to think about anything except the evening ahead of them. For this one night she wanted to put the painful past behind them—wipe out the memory of the last three lonely years.

She could see Evan waiting for her when she arrived at the marina. The wind had turned brisk, perfect for sailing. The scent of salt and sea was carried on the breeze. Grabbing her purse, she trotted across the parking lot. Evan reached for her hand as if doing so was an everyday occurrence. Unthinkingly, Mary Jo gave it to him.

Both seemed to realize in the same instant what they'd done. Evan turned to her, his eyes questioning, as if he expected her to remove her hand from his. She met his gaze evenly and offered him a bright smile.

"I brought us something to eat," he said. "I don't know about you, but I'm starved."

Mary Jo was about to make some comment about his not eating an adequate lunch, when she remembered he'd been out with Catherine Moore. Mary Jo wondered if the other woman was as elegant as her name suggested.

Evan leapt aboard, then helped her onto the small deck. He went below to retrieve the jib and mainsail, and when he emerged Mary Jo asked, "Do you want me to rig the jib sail?"

He seemed surprised and pleased by the offer.

"That was the first thing you taught me, remember? I distinctly recall this long lecture about the importance of the captain and the responsibilities of the crew. Naturally, you were the distinguished skipper and I was the lowly crew."

Evan laughed and the sound floated out to sea on the tail end of a breeze. "You remember all that, do you?"

"Like it was yesterday."

"Then have a go," he said, motioning toward the mast. But he didn't actually leave all the work to her. They both moved forward and attached the stay for the jib to the mast, working together as if they'd been partners for years. When they were finished, Evan motored the sleek sailboat out of the slot and toward the open waters of Boston Harbor.

For all her earlier claims about not being a natural sailor, Mary Jo was still astonished by how much she'd enjoyed her times on the water. Her fondest memories of Evan had revolved around the hours spent aboard his boat. There was something wildly romantic about sailing together, gliding across the open water with the wind in their faces. She would always treasure those times with Evan.

Once they were safely out of the marina, they raised the mainsail and sliced through the emerald-green waters toward Massachusetts Bay.

"So you've been talking to Jessica, have you?" he asked with a casualness that didn't deceive her.

"Mostly I've been working for you," she countered. "That doesn't leave me much time for socializing."

The wind whipped Evan's hair about his face, and he squinted into the sun. From the way he pinched his lips together, she guessed he was thinking about her date with Gary that weekend. She considered telling him it was over between her and Gary, but before she'd figured out a way of bringing up the subject, Evan spoke again.

"There's a bucket of fried chicken below," he mentioned with a knowing grin, "if you're hungry, that is."

"Fried chicken," she repeated. She had no idea why sailing made her ravenous. And Evan was well aware of her weakness for southern-fried chicken. "Made with a secret recipe of nine special herbs and spices? Plus coleslaw and french fries?"

Evan wiggled his eyebrows and smiled wickedly. "I seem to remember you had a fondness for a certain brand of chicken. There's a bottle of Chardonnay to go with it."

Mary Jo didn't need a second invitation to hurry below. She loaded up their plates, collected the bottle and two wineglasses and carefully carried everything up from the galley.

Sitting next to Evan, her plate balanced on her knees, she ate her dinner, savoring every bite. She must have been more enthusiastic than she realized, because she noticed him studying her. With a chicken leg poised in front of her mouth, she looked back at him.

"What's wrong?"

He grinned. "Nothing. I appreciate a woman who enjoys her food, that's all."

"I'll have you know I skipped lunch." But she wasn't going to tell him it was because every time she thought about him with Catherine Moore, she lost her appetite.

"I hope your employer values your dedication."

"I hope he does, too."

When they'd finished, Mary Jo carried their plates below and packed everything neatly away.

She returned and sat next to Evan. They finished their wine, then he allowed her a turn at the helm. Almost before she was aware of it, his arms were around her. She stood there, hardly breathing, then allowed herself to lean back against his chest. It was as if three painful years had been obliterated and they were both so much in love they couldn't see anything beyond the stars in their eyes.

Those had been innocent days for Mary Jo, that summer when she'd actually believed that an electrician's daughter could fit into the world of a man as rich and influential as Evan Dryden.

If she closed her eyes, she could almost forget everything that had happened since...

The wind blew more strongly and dusk settled over the water. Mary Jo realized with intense regret that it was time for them to head back to the marina. Evan seemed to feel the same unwillingness to return to land—and reality.

They were both quiet as they docked. Working together, they removed and stowed the sails.

Once everything was locked up, Evan walked her to the dimly lighted parking area. Mary Jo stood by the driver's side of her small car, reluctant to leave.

"I had a wonderful time," she whispered. "Thank you."

"I had a good time, too. Perhaps *too* good."

Mary Jo knew what he was saying; she felt it herself. It would be so easy to forget the past and pick up where they'd left off. Without much encouragement, she could easily find herself in his arms.

When he'd held her those few minutes on the boat, she'd experienced a feeling of warmth and completeness. Of happiness.

Sadness settled over her now, the weight of it almost unbearable. "Thank you again." She turned away and with a trembling hand inserted the car key into the lock. She wished Evan would leave before she did something ridiculous, like break into tears.

"Would you come sailing with me again some time?" he asked, and Mary Jo could have sworn he sounded tentative, uncertain. Which was ridiculous. Evan was one of the most supremely confident men she'd ever known.

Mary Jo waited for an objection to present itself. Several did. But not a single one of them seemed worth worrying about. Not tonight...

"I'd enjoy that very much." It was odd to be carrying on a conversation with her back to him, but she didn't dare turn around for fear she'd throw herself into his arms.

"Soon," he suggested, his voice low.

"How soon?"

"Next Saturday afternoon."

She swallowed against the constriction in her throat and nodded. "What time?"

"Noon. Meet me here, and we'll have lunch first."

"All right."

From the light sound of his footsteps, she knew he'd moved away. "Evan," she called, whirling around, her heart racing.

He turned toward her and waited for her to speak.

"Are you sure?" Mary Jo felt as if her heart hung in the balance.

His face was half-hidden by shadows, but she could see the smile that slowly grew. "I'm very sure."

Mary Jo's hands shook as she climbed into her car. It was happening all over again and she was *letting* it happen. She was trembling so badly she could hardly fasten her seat belt.

What did she hope to prove? She already *knew* that nothing she could do would make her the right woman for Evan. Eventually she would have to face the painful truth—again—and walk away from him. Eventually she would have to look him in the eye and tell him she couldn't be part of his life.

Mary Jo didn't sleep more than fifteen minutes at a stretch that night. When the alarm sounded, her eyes burned, her head throbbed and she felt as lifeless as the dish of last week's pasta still sitting in her fridge.

She climbed out of bed, showered and put on the first outfit she pulled out of her closet. Then she downed a cup of coffee and two aspirin.

Evan was already at the office when she arrived. "Good morning," he said cheerfully as she walked in the door.

"Morning."

"Beautiful day, isn't it?"

Mary Jo hadn't noticed. She sat down at her desk and stared at the blank computer screen.

Evan brought her a cup of coffee and she blinked up at him. "I thought I was the one who was supposed to make the coffee."

"I got here a few minutes early," he explained. "Drink up. You look like you could use it."

Despite her misery, she found the strength to grin. "I could."

"What's the matter? Bad night?"

She cupped the steaming mug with both hands. "Something like that." She couldn't very well confess *he* was the reason she hadn't slept. "Give me a few minutes and I'll be fine." A few minutes to scrounge up the courage to tell him she had other plans for Saturday and couldn't meet him, after all. A few minutes to control the searing disappointment. A few minutes to remind herself she could survive without him. The past three years had proved that.

"Let me know if there's anything I can get you."

She was about to suggest an appointment with a psychiatrist, then changed her mind. Evan would think she was joking; Mary Jo wasn't so sure it *was* a joke. Who else would put herself through this kind of torture?

"I've already sorted through the mail," Evan announced. "There's something here from Adison Investments."

That bit of information perked Mary Jo up. "What did they say?"

"I haven't read it yet, but as soon as I do, I'll let you know. I'm hoping my letter persuaded Adison to agree to a refund."

"That's what you hope, not what you expect."

Evan's dark eyes were serious. "Yes."

He returned to his office but was back out almost immediately. Shaking his head, he handed Mary Jo the brief letter. She read the two curt paragraphs and felt a sinking sense of discouragement. She had to hand it to Bill Adison. He was smooth. Believable. He had to be, otherwise her father would never have trusted him. Adison reiterated that he had a signed contract and that the initial investment wouldn't be returned until the terms of their agreement had been fully met. Never mind that he hadn't upheld *his* side of the contract.

"Do you want to make an appointment with my parents?" she asked, knowing Evan would want to discuss the contents of the letter with her mother and father.

Evan took several moments to consider the question. "No. I think it'd be better for me to stop off at their house myself and explain it to them. Less formal that way."

"Fine," she said, praying he wouldn't suggest Sunday. If he arrived Sunday afternoon, one or more of her family members would be sure to tell him she'd broken up with Gary. No doubt her niece Sally would blurt out that Evan could marry her now.

"I should probably talk to them today or tomorrow."

Mary Jo nodded, trying to conceal her profound relief.

"Why don't we plan on stopping by this evening after work?"

The "we" part didn't escape her.

"I'll call my folks and tell them," she said, figuring she'd set a time with them and then—later—make some plausible excuse for not joining Evan. Like a previous date. Or an emergency appointment with a manicurist. She'd break one of her nails and...

She was being ridiculous. She *should* be there. She *would* be there. She owed it to her parents. And it was business, after all, not a social excursion with Evan. Or a real date. There was nothing to fear.

Mary Jo had just arrived at this conclusion when Evan called her into his office.

"Feeling better?" he asked, closing the door behind her.

"A little." She managed a tremulous smile.

He stared at her for an uncomfortable moment. She would have walked around him and seated herself, but he blocked the way.

"I know what might help," he said after a moment.

Thinking he was going to suggest aspirin, Mary Jo opened her mouth to tell him she'd already taken some. Before she could speak, he removed the pen and pad from her unresisting fingers and set them aside.

"What are you doing?" she asked, frowning in confusion.

He grinned almost boyishly. "Mary Jo, I am, as they say in the movies, about to kiss you senseless."

CHAPTER SIX

"YOU'RE GOING TO KISS ME?" Mary Jo's heart lurched as Evan drew her into his arms. His breath felt warm against her face, and a wonderful, wicked feeling spread through her. She sighed and closed her eyes.

Evan eased his mouth over hers and it felt so natural, so familiar. So right.

He kissed her again, and tears gathered in Mary Jo's eyes. He wrapped her tightly in his arms and took several long, deep breaths.

"I wanted to do this last night," he whispered.

She'd wanted him to kiss her then, too, yet—paradoxically—she'd been grateful he hadn't. It occurred to her now that delaying this moment could have been a mistake. They'd both thought about it, wondered how it would be, anticipated being in each other's arms again. And after all that intense speculation, their kiss might have disappointed them both.

It hadn't.

Nevertheless, Mary Jo was relieved when the phone rang. Evan cursed under his breath. "We need to talk about this," he muttered, still holding her.

The phone pealed a second time.

"We'll talk later," she promised quickly.

Evan released her, and she leapt for the telephone on his desk. Thankfully, the call was for Evan. Thankfully, it wasn't Jessica. Or her mother. Or Gary.

Mary Jo left his office and sank slowly into her chair. Closing her eyes, she tried to make sense of what had happened.

All too soon Evan was back. He sat on the edge of her desk. "All right," he said, his eyes as bright and happy as a schoolboy's on the first day of summer vacation. "We're going to have this out once and for all."

"Have this out?"

"I don't know what happened between you and the man you fell in love with three years ago. But apparently it didn't work out, which is fine with me."

"Evan, please!" She glanced desperately around. "Not here. Not now." She was shaking inside. Her stomach knotted and her chest hurt with the effort of holding back her emotions. Eventually she'd have to tell Evan there'd never been another man, but she wasn't looking forward to admitting that lie. Or her reasons for telling it.

"You're right." He sounded, reluctant as if he wanted to settle everything between them then and there. "This isn't the place. We need to be able to talk freely." He looked at his watch and his mouth tightened. "I've got to be in court this morning."

"Yes, I know." She was pathetically grateful that he'd be out of the office for a few hours. She needed time to think. She'd already made one decision, though: she refused to lie to him again. She was older now, more mature, and she recognized that, painful though it was, Evan's mother had been right. Mary Jo could do nothing to enhance Evan's career.

But she wasn't going to run away and hide, the way she had three years ago. Nor could she bear the thought of pitting Evan against his parents. The Drydens were a close family, like her own. No, she'd have to find some other approach, some other way of convincing him this relationship couldn't possibly work. Just *how* she was going to do this, she had no idea.

Pulling her thoughts back to her morning tasks, she reached for the mail and quickly became absorbed in her work. In fact, she was five minutes late meeting Jessica.

Her friend was waiting in the Italian restaurant, sitting at a table in the back. A grandmotherly woman was holding Andy, using a bread stick to entertain the toddler.

"Nonna, this is my friend Mary Jo," Jessica said when she approached the table.

"Hello," Mary Jo murmured, pulling out a chair.

"Leave lunch to me," Nonna insisted, giving Andy back to his mother, who placed him in the high chair beside her. Jessica then handed her son another bread stick, which delighted him. Apparently Andy didn't understand he was supposed to *eat* the bread. He seemed to think it was a toy to wave gleefully overhead, and Mary Jo found herself cheered by his antics.

The older woman returned with large bowls of minestrone, plus a basket of bread so fresh it was still warm. "You eat now," she instructed, waiting for them to sample the delectable-smelling soup. "Enjoy your food first. You can talk later."

"It would be impossible *not* to enjoy our food," Jessica told Nonna, who beamed with pride.

"Nonna's right, of course," Jessica said, "but we've got less than an hour and I'm dying to hear what's happening with you and Evan."

"Not much." Which was sort of the truth. For now. Mary Jo described how Evan had coerced her into working for him. She'd expected expressions of sympathy from her friend. Instead, Jessica seemed downright pleased.

"Damian said there'd been some misunderstanding about a file. He said Evan had suspected you of doing something underhanded, and when Damian showed up with it, Evan felt wretched."

"That's all behind us now." The uncertainty of their future loomed before them, and that was what concerned her most. Mary Jo weighed the decision to confide in Jessica about their kiss that morning. If Jessica were someone other than Evan's sister-in-law, she might have done so. But it would be unfair to involve his family in this.

Jessica dipped her spoon into the thick soup. "I explained earlier that Evan and I became fairly close while I was working for the firm. What I didn't mention was how often he talked about you. He really loved you, Mary Jo."

Uncomfortable, Mary Jo lowered her gaze.

"I'm not saying this to make you feel guilty, but so you'll know that Evan's feelings for you were genuine. You weren't just a passing fancy to him. In some ways, I don't believe he's ever gotten over you."

Mary Jo nearly choked on her soup. "I wish that was true. I've arranged no less than six luncheon appointments for him. All the names came directly out of his little black book. The invitations were accompanied by a dozen red roses." Until that moment, Mary Jo hadn't realized how jealous she was, and how much she'd been suffering while he'd wined and dined his girlfriends.

"Don't get me wrong," Jessica said. "Evan's dated. But there's never been anyone serious."

Mary Jo energetically ripped off a piece of bread. "He's gone out of his way to prove otherwise."

"What were these women's names?"

Nonna returned to the table with a large platter heaped with marinated vegetables, sliced meats and a variety of cheeses. Andy stretched out his hand, wanting a piece of cheese, which Jessica willingly gave him.

"One was Catherine Moore."

A smile hovered at the edges of Jessica's mouth. "Catherine Moore is close to seventy and she's his great-aunt."

Shocked, Mary Jo jerked up her head. "His great-aunt? What about..." and she rolled off the other names she remembered.

"All relatives," Jessica said, shaking her head. "The poor boy was desperate to make you jealous."

Mary Jo had no intention of admitting how well his scheme had worked. "Either that, or he was being thoughtful," she suggested offhandedly—just to be fair to Evan. She wanted to be angry with him, but found she was more amused.

"Trust me," Jessica said, smiling broadly. "Evan was desperate. He's dated, true, but he seldom goes out with the same woman more than three or four times. His mother's beginning to wonder if he'll ever settle down.''

At the mention of Lois Dryden, Mary Jo paid close attention to her soup. ''It was my understanding that Evan was planning to go into politics.''

''I believe he will someday,'' Jessica answered enthusiastically. ''In my opinion, he should. Evan has a generous, caring heart. He genuinely wants to help people. More important, he's the kind of man who's capable of finding solutions and making a difference.

''He's a wonderful diplomat, and people like him. It doesn't matter what walk of life they're from either. The best way I can describe it is that Evan's got charisma.''

Mary Jo nodded. It was the truth.

''Although he went into corporate law,'' Jessica continued, ''I don't think his heart has ever really been in it. You should have seen him when he represented Earl Kress. He was practically a different person. No, I don't think he's at all happy as a corporate attorney.''

''Then why hasn't he decided to run for office?''

''I don't know,'' Jessica answered thoughtfully. ''I assumed, for a while, that he was waiting until he was a bit older, but I doubt that's the reason. I know his family encourages him, especially his mother. Lois has always believed Evan's destined for great things.''

''I . . . got that impression from her, as well.''

''Evan and Damian have had long talks about his running for office. Damian's encouraged him, too, but Evan says the time's not right.''

Mary Jo's heart felt heavy. Everything Jessica said seconded Lois Dryden's concerns about the role Evan's wife would play in his future.

"You're looking thoughtful."

Mary Jo forced a small smile. "I never understood what it was about me that attracted Evan."

"I know exactly what it was," Jessica said without a pause. "He told me himself, and more than once. He said it was as though you knew him inside and out. Apparently you could see right through his schemes. I suspect it has something to do with the fact that you have five older brothers."

"Probably."

"Evan's been able to charm his way around just about everyone. Not you. You laughed at him and told him to save his breath on more than one occasion. Am I right?"

Mary Jo nodded, remembering the first day they'd met on the beach. He'd tried to sweet-talk her into a dinner date, and she'd refused. It didn't take much for her to realize that Evan Dryden didn't know how to accept no for an answer. In the end they'd compromised. They'd built a small fire, roasted hot dogs and marshmallows and sat on the beach talking until well past midnight.

They saw each other regularly after that. Mary Jo knew he was wealthy by the expensive sports car he drove, the kind of money he flashed around. In the beginning she'd assumed it was simply because he was a high-priced attorney. Fool that she'd been, Mary Jo hadn't even recognized the name.

It wasn't until much later, after she was already head over heels in love with him, that she learned the truth.

Evan was more than wealthy. He came from a family whose history stretched back to the *Mayflower*.

"You were different from the other women he'd known," Jessica was saying. "He could be himself with you. One time he told me he felt an almost spiritual connection with you. It was something he never expected to find with anyone else."

"Evan told you all that?" Mary Jo asked breathlessly.

"Yes, and much more," Jessica said, leaning forward. "You see, Mary Jo, I know how much Evan loved you—and still loves you."

Mary Jo felt as if she was about to break into deep, racking sobs. She loved Evan, too. Perhaps there *was* hope for them. Jessica made her feel they might have a future. She seemed to have such faith that, whatever their problems, love and understanding could work them out.

Mary Jo returned to the office, her heart full of hope. She'd been wrong not to believe in their love, wrong not to give them a chance. Her insecurities had wasted precious years.

When Evan walked in, it was close to five o'clock. Mary Jo resisted the urge to fly into his arms, but immediately sensed something was wrong. He was frowning and every line of his body was tense.

"What happened?" she asked, following him into his office.

"I lost," he said pacing. "You know something? I'm a damn poor loser."

She *had* noticed, but he hadn't experienced losses often enough to grow accustomed to accepting them.

"Listen, it happens to the best of us," she assured him.

"But it shouldn't have in this case. We were in the right."

"You win some and you lose some. That's the nature of the legal game."

He glared at her and she laughed outright. He reminded her of one of her brothers after a highly contested high-school basketball game. Mark, the youngest, had always loved sports and was fiercely competitive. He'd had to be in order to compete against his four brothers. In many ways, Evan reminded her of Mark.

"I can always count on you to soothe my battered ego, can't I?" he asked, his tone more than a little sarcastic.

"No. You can always count on me to tell you the truth." *Almost always,* she amended sadly, recalling her one lie.

"A kiss would make me feel better."

"Certainly not," she said briskly, but it was difficult to refuse him anything. "Not here, anyway."

"You're right," he admitted grudgingly, "but at least let me hold you." She wasn't given the opportunity to refuse, not that she would have found the strength to do so.

He brought her into his arms and held her firmly against him, breathing deeply as if to absorb everything about her. "I can't believe I'm holding you like this," he whispered.

"Neither will anyone else who walks into this room." But she didn't care who saw them. She burrowed deeper into his embrace and rested her head against the solid strength of his chest.

He eased himself away from her and framed her face with his hands. His eyes were intense as he gazed down on her. "I don't care about the past, Mary Jo. It's water under the bridge. None of it matters. The only thing that matters is *right now*. Can we put everything else behind us and move forward?"

She bit her lower lip, her heart full of a new confidence. Nothing in this world would ever stand between them again. She would have said the words, but couldn't speak, so she nodded her head in abrupt little movements.

She found herself pulled back in his arms, the embrace so hard it threatened to cut off her breath, but she didn't care. Breathing hardly seemed necessary when Evan was holding her like this. She wanted to laugh and to weep both at once, to throw back her head and shout with a free-flowing joy that sprang from her soul.

"We'll go to your parents' place," Evan said, "talk to them about Adison's response, and then I'll take you to dinner and from there—"

"Stop," Mary Jo said, breaking free of his hold and raising her right hand. "You'll take me to dinner? Do you honestly believe we're going to escape my mother without being fed?"

Evan laughed and pulled her back into the circle of his arms. "I suppose not."

Evan was, of course, welcomed enthusiastically by both her parents. He and Norman Summerhill discussed the Adison situation, while Mary Jo helped her mother prepare a simple meal of fried chicken and a pasta and vegetable salad. Over dinner, the mood was comfortable and light-hearted.

As it turned out, though, the evening included a lot more than just conversation and dinner. Her brothers all played on a softball team. They had a game scheduled for that evening, and one of the other players had injured his ankle in a fall at work. The instant Evan heard the news, he volunteered to substitute.

"Evan," Mary Jo pleaded. "This isn't like handball, you know. These guys take their game seriously."

"You think handball isn't serious?" Evan kissed her on the nose and left her with her parents while he hurried home to change clothes.

Her mother watched from the kitchen, looking exceptionally pleased. She wiped her hands on her apron skirt. "I think you did a wise thing breaking up with Gary when you did."

"I'm so happy, Mom," Mary Jo whispered, grabbing a dish towel and some plates to dry.

"You love him."

Mary Jo noticed it wasn't a question.

"I never stopped loving him."

Her mother placed one arm around Mary Jo's slender shoulders. "I knew that the minute I saw the two of you together again." She paused, apparently considering her next words. "I've always known you loved Evan. Can you tell me what happened before—why you broke it off?"

"I didn't believe I was the right woman for him."

"Nonsense! Anyone looking at the two of you would realize you're perfect for each other. Who would say such a thing to you?"

Mary Jo was intelligent enough not to mention Lois Dryden. "He's very wealthy, Mom."

"You can look past that."

Mary Jo's laugh was spontaneous. Her sweetheart of a mother saw Evan's money as a detriment—and in some ways, it was.

"His father's a senator."

"You think his money bought him that position?" Marianna scoffed. "If you do, you're wrong. He was elected to that office because he's a decent man with an honest desire to help his constituents."

Her mother had a way of making the impossible sound plausible. Mary Jo wished she could be more like her.

"Now, freshen up," Marianna said, untying the apron, "or we'll be late for your brothers' softball game."

Evan was already in the outfield catching fly balls when Mary Jo and her parents arrived. He looked as if he'd been a member of the team for years.

The game was an exciting one, with the outcome unpredictable until the very end of the ninth inning. Mary Jo, sitting in the bleachers with her family—her parents, a couple of sisters-in-law, some nieces and nephews—screamed herself hoarse. Their team lost by one run, but everyone took the defeat in stride—including Evan, who'd played as hard as any of them.

Afterward, the team went out for pizza and cold beer. Mary Jo joined Evan and the others, while her parents returned to the house, tired out from the excitement.

Evan threw his arm over her shoulders and she wrapped her own arm around his waist.

"You two an item now or something?" her brother Bill asked as they gathered around a long table at the pizza parlor.

"Yeah," Rich chimed in. "You two look awful chummy all of a sudden. What's going on?"

"Yeah, what about good ol' Gary?" Mark wanted to know.

Evan studied her, eyebrows raised. "What *about* Gary?" he echoed.

"You don't need to worry about him anymore," Jack explained, carrying a pitcher of ice-cold beer to the table. "M.J. broke up with him over the weekend."

"You did?" It was Evan who asked the question.

"Yup." Once more her brother was doing the talking for her. "Said they were drifting in opposite directions or some such garbage. No one believed her. We know the *real* reason she showed Gary the door."

"Will you guys *please stop?*" Mary Jo insisted, her ears growing redder by the minute. "I can speak for myself, thank you very much."

Jack poured them each a glass of beer and slid them down the table. "You know M.J. means business when she says *please stop.* Uh-oh—look at her ears. Let's not embarrass her anymore, guys, or there'll be hell to pay later."

Evan barked with laughter, and her brothers looked on approvingly. He fit in with her family as if he'd been born into it. This was his gift, Mary Jo realized. He was completely at ease with her brothers—as he would be with a group of government officials or lawyers or "society" people. With *anyone*. He could drink beer and enjoy it as much as expensive cham-

pagne. It didn't matter to him if he ate pizza or lob-
ster.

But Mary Jo was definitely more comfortable with
the pizza-and-beer way of life. Hours earlier she'd
been utterly confident. Now, for the first time that
night, her newfound resolve was shaken.

Evan seemed to notice it, although he didn't say
anything until later, when they were alone, driving to
her place. Reluctant for the evening to end, Mary Jo
gazed at the oncoming lights of the cars zooming past.
She couldn't suppress a sigh.

Evan glanced over at her. "Your family's wonderful," he said conversationally. "I envy you coming
from such a large, close-knit group."

"You're close to your brother, too."

"True. More so now that we're older." He reached
for her hand and squeezed it gently. "Something's
troubling you."

She stared out the side window. "You're comfortable in my world, Evan, but I'm not comfortable in
yours."

"World? What are you talking about? In case you
haven't noticed, we're both right here in the same
world—earth."

She smiled, knowing he was making light of her
concerns. "If we'd been with your family, do you seriously think we'd be having pizza and beer? More
than likely it'd be expensive French wine, baguettes
and Brie."

"So? You don't like baguettes and Brie?"

"Yes, but . . ." She paused, knowing it wouldn't do
any good to argue. He didn't understand her con-

cerns, because he didn't share them. "We're different, Evan."

"Thank goodness. I'd hate to think I was attracted to a clone of myself."

"I'm an electrician's daughter."

"A very lovely one, too, I might add."

"Evan," she groaned. "Be serious."

"I *am* serious. It'd scare the socks off you if you knew *how* serious."

He exited the freeway and headed down the street toward her duplex. As he parked, he said, "Invite me in for coffee."

"Are you really interested in coffee?"

"No."

"That's what I thought," she said, smiling softly to herself.

"I'm going to kiss you, Mary Jo, and frankly, I'm a little too old to be doing it in a car. Now invite me inside—or suffer the consequences."

Mary Jo didn't need a second invitation. Evan helped her out of the car and took her arm as they walked to her door. She unlocked it but didn't turn on the lights as they moved into her living room. The instant the door was closed, Evan turned her in his arms so that her back was pressed against it.

Her lips trembled as his mouth sought hers. It was a gentle caress rather than a kiss, and she moaned, wanting, *needing* more of him.

Evan's hand curved around the side of her neck, his fingers stroking her hair. His mouth hovered a fraction of an inch from hers, as if he half expected her to protest his kiss. Instead, she raised her head to meet his lips again.

Groaning, Evan kissed her with a passion that left her breathless and weak-kneed.

Mary Jo wound her arms around his neck and stood on the tips of her toes as his mouth worked hungrily over hers. They exchanged a series of long kisses, then Evan buried his head in her shoulder and shuddered.

Mary Jo was convinced that if he hadn't been holding her upright, she would have slithered to the floor.

"We'd better stop while I have the strength," Evan whispered, almost as if he was speaking more to himself than to her. His breathing was ragged and uneven. He moved away from her, and in the dark stillness of her living room, illumined only by the glow of a streetlight, she watched him rake his hands through his thick, dark hair.

"I'll make us that coffee," she said in a purposeful voice. They both squinted when she flipped on the light.

"I really don't need any coffee," he told her.

"I know. I don't, either. It's a convenient excuse for you to stay."

Evan followed her into the kitchen and pulled out a chair. He sat down and reached for her, wrapping his arms around her waist, pulling her down onto his lap. "We have a lot of time to make up for."

Unsure how to respond, Mary Jo rested her hands lightly on his shoulders. It was so easy to get caught up again in the intensity of their attraction and renewed love. But despite her earlier optimism, she couldn't allow herself to ignore the truth. Except that she didn't know how to resolve this, or even if she could.

Evan left soon afterward, with a good-night kiss and the reminder that they'd be together again in the morning.

Mary Jo sat in her rocking chair in the dark for a long time, trying to sort out her tangled thoughts. Loving him the way she did, it was so tempting to let her heart go where it wanted to. So tempting to throw caution to the winds, to ignore all the difficult questions.

Evan seemed confident that their love was possible. Jessica did, too. Mary Jo desperately wanted to believe them. She wanted to overlook every objection. She wanted what she would probably never receive—his family's approval. Not Damian and Jessica's; she had that. His mother and father's.

Sometimes loving someone wasn't enough. Mary Jo had heard that often enough and she recognized the truth of it.

Too tired to think clearly, she stood, setting the rocker into motion, and stumbled into her bedroom.

SATURDAY, MARY JO MET Evan at the yacht club at noon. They planned to sail after a leisurely lunch. She'd been looking forward to this from the moment Evan had invited her on Wednesday.

The receptionist ushered her to a table outside on the patio where Evan was waiting for her. There was a festive, summery atmosphere—tables with their striped red-yellow-and-blue umbrellas, the cheerful voices of other diners, the breathtaking view of the marina. Several sailboats with multicolored spinnakers could be seen against a backdrop of bright blue sky and sparkling green sea.

Evan stood as she approached and pulled out her chair. "I don't think you've ever looked more beautiful."

It was a line he'd used a thousand times before, Mary Jo was sure of that, although he sounded sincere. "You say that to all your dates," she chided lightly, reaching for the menu.

"But it's true," he returned with an injured air.

Mary Jo laughed and spread the linen napkin across her lap. "Your problem is that you're a wonderful liar. You'd be perfect in politics since you lie so convincingly." She'd been teasing, then suddenly realized how rude that sounded. His father was a politician!

"Oh, Evan, I'm sorry. That was a terrible thing to say." Mary Jo felt dreadful, and realized anew that she was the type of person who could offend someone without ever being aware of it. She simply wasn't circumspect enough.

He chuckled and brushed off her apology. "Dad would get a laugh out of what you said."

"Promise me you won't ever tell him."

"That depends," he said, paying exaggerated attention to his menu.

"On what?" she demanded.

He wiggled his eyebrows. "On what you intend to offer me for my silence."

She smiled and repeated a line her brothers had often used on her. "I'll let you live."

Evan threw back his head and laughed boisterously.

"Evan?" The woman's voice came from behind Mary Jo. "What a pleasant surprise to find you here."

"Mother," Evan said, standing to greet Lois Dryden. He kissed her on the cheek. "You remember Mary Jo Summerhill, don't you?"

CHAPTER SEVEN

"OF COURSE I REMEMBER Mary Jo," Lois Dryden said cheerfully. "How nice to see you again."

Mary Jo blinked, wondering if this was the same woman she'd had that painful heart-to-heart chat with all those years ago. The woman who'd suggested that if Mary Jo really loved Evan she would call off their engagement. Not in those words exactly. Mrs. Dryden had been far too subtle for that. Nevertheless, the message had been there, loud and clear.

"I didn't know you two were seeing each other again," Lois continued. "This is a . . . surprise."

Mary Jo noticed she didn't say it was *pleasant* surprise. Naturally, Evan's mother was much too polite to cause even a hint of a scene. Not at the yacht club, at any rate. Now, if she'd been at Whispering Willows, the Dryden estate, she might swoon or have a fit of vapors, or whatever it was wealthy women did to reveal their shock and displeasure. Mary Jo realized she was being cynical, but couldn't help herself.

Evan reached for her hand and clasped it in his own. His eyes smiled into hers. "Mary Jo's working for me this summer."

"I . . . I didn't know that."

"Would you care to join us?" Evan asked, but his eyes didn't waver from Mary Jo's. Although he'd issued the invitation, it was obvious that he expected his mother to refuse. That he *wanted* her to refuse.

"Another time, perhaps. I'm lunching with Jessica's mother. We're planning a first-birthday party celebration for Andrew, and, well, you know how the two of us feel about our only grandchild."

Evan chuckled. "I sure do. It seems to me that either Damian or I should see about adding another branch to the family tree."

Mary Jo felt the heat of embarrassment redden her ears. Evan couldn't have been more blatant. He'd all but announced he intended to marry her. She waited for his mother to comment.

"That would be lovely, Evan," Lois said, but if Evan didn't catch the tinge of disapproval in his mother's voice, Mary Jo did. Nothing had changed.

The lines were drawn.

Lois made her excuses and hurried back into the yacht club. Mary Jo's good mood plummeted. She made a pretense of enjoying her lunch and decided to put the small confrontation behind her. Her heart was set on enjoying this day with Evan. She loved sailing as much as he did, and as soon as they were out in the bay, she could forget how strongly his mother disapproved of her. *Almost* forget.

They worked together to get the sailboat in motion. Once the sails were raised, she sat next to Evan. The wind tossed her hair about her face, and she smiled into the warm, cheerful sunshine. They tacked left and then right, zigzagging their way through the water.

"Are you thirsty?" Evan asked after they'd been out for about an hour.

"A cold soda sounds good."

"Great. While you're in the galley, would you get one for me?"

Laughing, she jabbed him in the ribs for the clever way he'd tricked her into getting his drink. She went below and brought back two sodas. She handed him his, then reclaimed her spot beside him.

Evan eased his arm around her shoulder and soon she was nestled against him, guiding the sailboat, with Evan guiding her. When she veered off course and the sails slackened, he placed his hand over hers and gently steered them back on course.

Mary Jo had found it easy to talk to Evan from the moment they'd met. He was easygoing and congenial, open-minded and witty. But this afternoon he seemed unusually quiet. She wondered if he was thinking about the unexpected encounter with his mother.

"It's peaceful, isn't it?" Mary Jo said after several long moments of silence.

"I think some of the most profound moments of my life have been spent aboard this boat. I've always come here to find peace, and I have, though it's usually been hard won."

"I'm grateful you introduced me to sailing."

"I took the boat out several times after...three years ago." His hold on her tightened slightly. "I've missed you, Mary Jo," he whispered, and rubbed the side of his jaw against her temple. "My world felt so empty without you."

"Mine did, too," she admitted softly, remembering the bleak, empty months after their breakup.

"Earl Kress stopped off at the office a while back, and I learned you weren't married. Afterward, I couldn't get you out of my mind. I wondered what had happened between you and this teacher you loved. I wanted to contact you and find out. I must have come up with a hundred schemes to worm my way back into your life."

"W-why didn't you?" She felt comfortable and secure in his arms, unafraid of the problems that had driven them apart. She could deal with the past; it was the future that terrified her.

"Pride mostly," Evan said quietly. "A part of me was hoping you'd eventually come back to me."

In a way she had, on her knees, needing him. Funny, she couldn't have approached him for herself, even though she was madly in love with him, but she'd done it for her parents.

"No wonder you had that gleeful look in your eye when I walked into your office," she said, hiding a smile. "You'd been waiting for that very thing."

"I wanted to punish you," he told her, and she heard the regret in his voice. "I wanted to make you suffer the way I had. That was the reason I insisted you work for me this summer. I'd already hired Mrs. Sterling's replacement, but when I had the opportunity to force you into accepting the position, I couldn't resist."

This wasn't news to Mary Jo. She'd known the moment he'd offered her the job what his intention was. He wanted to make her as miserable as she'd made him. And his plan worked those first few days. She'd gone home frustrated, mentally beaten and physically exhausted.

"A woman of lesser fortitude would have quit the first day, when you had me ordering roses and booking luncheon dates."

"Those weren't any love interests," he confessed. "I'm related to each one."

"I know." She tilted back her head and kissed the underside of his jaw.

"How?" he asked, his surprise evident.

"Jessica told me."

"Well, I certainly hope you were jealous. I went through a great deal of unnecessary trouble if you weren't."

"I was green with it." She could have downplayed her reaction, but didn't. "Every time you left the office for another one of your dates, I worked myself into a frenzy. Please, Evan, don't ever do that to me again."

"I won't," he promised, and she could feel his smile against her hair. "But you had your revenge several times over, throwing Gary in my face. I disliked the man from the moment we met. Here I was, hoping to catch you off guard by showing up at your parents' for dinner, and my plan immediately backfires when you arrive with your boyfriend in tow."

"You didn't like Gary?"

"He's probably a nice guy, but not when he's dating *my* woman."

"But you acted like Gary was an old pal! I was mortified. My entire family thought it was hilarious. You had more to say to Gary than to me."

"I couldn't let you know how jealous I was, could I?"

Mary Jo snuggled more securely in his arms. A sea gull's cry sounded from overhead, and she looked into the brilliant blue sky, reveling in the sunshine and the breeze and in the rediscovery of their love.

"Can we ever go back?" Evan asked. "Is it possible to pretend those years didn't happen and take up where we left off?"

"I . . . I don't know," Mary Jo whispered. Yet she couldn't keep her heart from hoping. She closed her eyes and felt the wind on her face. Those years had changed her. She was more confident now, more sure of herself, emotionally stronger. This time she'd fight harder to hold on to her happiness.

One thing was certain. If she walked out of Evan's life again, it wouldn't be in silence or in secrecy.

She remembered the pain of adjusting to her life without Evan. Pride had carried her for several months. She might not come from old Boston wealth, but she had nothing to be ashamed of. She was proud of her family and refused to apologize because they were working class.

But pride had only taken her so far, and when it had worn down, all that was left was the emptiness of her dreams and a life that felt hollow.

Like Evan, she'd forced herself to go on, dragging from one day to the next, but she wasn't fully alive and hadn't been until a few days ago, when he'd taken her in his arms and kissed her. Her love for him, her regret at what she'd lost, had refused to go away.

"I want to give us another chance," Evan murmured. The teasing had gone out of his voice. "Do you?"

"Yes. Oh, yes," Mary Jo said ardently.

He kissed her then, with a passion and a fervor she'd never experienced before. She returned his kiss in full measure. They clung tightly to each other until the sails flapped in the breeze and Evan had to grip the helm and steer them back on course.

"I love you, Mary Jo," Evan said. "Heaven knows, I tried not to. I became...rather irresponsible after we split up, you know. If it hadn't been for Damian, I don't know what I would have done. He was endlessly patient with me, even when I wouldn't tell him what was wrong. My brother isn't stupid. He knew it had something to do with you. I just couldn't talk about it. The only relief I found was here on the water."

Turning, Mary Jo wrapped her arms around his middle and pressed her face against his chest, wanting to absorb his pain.

"When you told me you'd fallen in love with another man, I was left with no recourse but to accept that it was over. I realized the moment you told me how difficult it was for you. Loving him while you were still engaged to me must have been hell."

A sob was trapped in her throat. This was the time to admit there'd never been another man, that it was all a lie....

"Can you tell me about him?"

"No." She jerked her head from side to side in adamant refusal. She couldn't do it, just couldn't do it. She was continuing the lie, Lord help her, but telling him would mean betraying his mother's part in all this. She wouldn't do that.

His free arm cradled her shoulders, his grip tight.

"I'd more or less decided that if I couldn't marry you," Evan said after a lengthy pause, "I wasn't getting married at all. Can't you just see me twenty years down the road sitting by a roaring fireplace in a smoking jacket with my ever-faithful dog sleeping at my side?"

The mental picture was so foreign to the devil-may-care image she'd had of him these past few years that she laughed out loud. "You in a smoking jacket? Never. You don't even smoke."

"What about me living in a huge, seven-bedroom house all by myself?"

"I can't picture that, either."

"What about fatherhood? Can you picture me as a father?"

"Easily." After watching him with Andrew and her own nieces and nephews, she realized Evan was a natural with children.

"Then it's settled," he said, sounding greatly relieved.

"What's settled?" she asked, cocking her head to one side to look up at him. His attention was focused straight ahead as he steered the sailboat.

"We're getting married. So, sweetheart, prepare yourself, because we're making up for lost time."

"Evan—"

"If you recall, when I first gave you the engagement ring, we planned our family. Remember? Right down to the timing of your first pregnancy."

Mary Jo could hardly manage a nod. Those were memories she'd rarely allowed herself to take out and examine.

"We both thought it was important to wait a couple of years before we started our family. You were supposed to have our first baby this year. Hey, we're already behind schedule! It seems to me we'd better take an extended honeymoon."

Mary Jo laughed, the wind swallowing the sound the moment it escaped her lips.

"Two, three months at the very least," Evan continued, undaunted. "I suggest a South Pacific island, off the tourist track. We'll rent a bungalow on the beach and spend our days walking along the shore and our nights making love."

He was going much too fast for her. "Do you mind retracing a few steps?" she asked. "I got lost somewhere between you sitting by a roaring fire with your faithful dog and us running into Gauguin's descendants on some South Pacific beach."

"First things first," Evan countered. "We agreed on four children, didn't we?"

"Evan!" She couldn't keep from laughing, her happiness spilling over.

"These details are important, and I want them settled before we get involved in another subject. I wanted six kids, remember. I love big families. But you only wanted two. If you'll think back, it took some fast talking to get you to agree to a compromise of four. You did agree, remember?"

"What I remember was being railroaded into a crazy conversation while you went on about building us this mansion."

"Ah, yes, the house. I'd nearly forgotten. I wanted one large enough for all the kids. With a couple of guest rooms. That, my beautiful Mary Jo, isn't a mansion."

"It is when you're talking seven bedrooms and six thousand square feet."

"But," Evan said, his eyes twinkling, "you were going to have live-in help with the children, especially while they're younger, and I wanted to be sure we had a place to escape and relax at the end of the day."

"I found an indoor swimming pool, hot tub and exercise room a bit extravagant." Mary Jo had thought he was teasing when he'd showed her the house plans he'd had drawn up, but it had soon become apparent that he was completely serious. He was serious now, too.

"I still want to build that home for us," he said, his intense dark eyes searching hers. "I love you. I've loved you for three agonizing years. I want us to be married, and soon. If it were up to me, we'd already have the marriage license."

"You're crazy." But it was a wonderful kind of crazy.

"You love me."

Tears glistened in her eyes as she nodded. "I do. I love you so much, Evan." She slid her arms around his neck. "What am I going to do with you?"

"Marry me and put me out of my misery."

He made it sound so easy and she was caught up in the tide of his enthusiasm, but she couldn't agree. Not yet. Not until she was convinced she was doing the right thing for both of them.

"Listen," Evan said as though struck by a whole new thought. "I have a judge in the family who can marry us as soon as I make the necessary arrangements. We can have a private ceremony in, say, three days' time.''

"My parents would shoot us both, Evan. I know for a fact that my father would never forgive us if we cheated him out of the pleasure of escorting me down the aisle.''

Evan grimaced. "You're right. My mother's the same. She actually enjoys planning social events. It's much worse now that my dad's a senator. She's organized to a fault—takes care of even the most minute details.'' He grinned suddenly, as if he found something amusing. "My father made a wise choice when he married Mom. She's the perfect politician's wife.''

The words cut through Mary Jo like an icy wind. They reminded her that she would be a liability to Evan should he ever decide to run for political office.

Often the candidates' spouses were put under as much scrutiny as the candidates themselves. The demands placed on political wives were often no less demanding than those placed on the politicians.

"Evan,'' she said, watching him closely. "I'm not anything like your mother.''

"So? What's that got to do with our building a mansion and filling all those bedrooms with children?''

"I won't make a good politician's wife.''

He looked at her as if he didn't understand what she was saying.

Mary Jo had no option but to elaborate. "I've heard, from various people, that you intend to enter politics someday yourself.''

"Someday. I'm in no rush. My family, my mother especially, seems to think I have a future in that area, but it isn't anything that's going to happen soon. When and if the time comes, the two of us will decide it together. But for now it's a moot point."

Mary Jo wasn't willing to accept that. "Evan, I'm telling you here and now that I'd hate that kind of life. I'm not suited for it. Your mother enjoys arranging spectacular society events and giving interviews and living her life a certain way, but I don't. I'm the kind of person who's uncomfortable in a roomful of strangers—unless they're five-year-olds."

"All right," Evan said with an amused air. "Then I won't enter politics. My mother has enough to keep her busy running my father's career. You're far more important to me than some elected position. Besides, I have the feeling Mother would have driven me crazy."

His words should have reassured her, but didn't. It seemed ludicrous to pin their future together on something as fleeting as this promise, so lightly made. Her greatest fear was that Evan would change his mind and regret ever marrying her.

"Let's go talk to your parents," Evan said, apparently unaware of the turmoil inside her.

"About what?"

His head went back and he frowned at her. "Making the arrangements for the wedding, what else? My mother will put up a fight, but I believe a small, private ceremony with just our immediate families would be best."

"Oh, Evan, please, don't rush me," Mary Jo pleaded. "This is the most important decision of our lives. We both need to think this through very carefully."

He gaze narrowed. "What's there to think about? I love you, and you love me. That's all that matters."

How Mary Jo wished that were true.

IT DEMANDED far more courage to drive over to Whispering Willows than Mary Jo anticipated. She'd spent most of the night alternating between absolute delight and abject despair. She awoke Sunday morning convinced she'd never find the answers she needed until she'd talked to Evan's mother.

That was how Mary Jo came to be standing outside the Drydens' front door shortly before noon. With a shaking hand, she rang the bell.

She'd expected one of the household staff to answer. Instead, Lois Dryden herself appeared at the door. The two women stared at each other.

Mary Jo recovered enough to speak first. "I'm sorry to disturb you, Mrs. Dryden, but I was wondering if I could have a few minutes of your time."

"Of course." The older woman stepped aside to let Mary Jo enter the lavish house. The foyer floor was of polished marble, and a glittering crystal chandelier hung from the ceiling, which was two and a half stories high.

"Perhaps it would be best if we talked in my husband's office," Lois Dryden said, ushering Mary Jo's to the darkly paneled room down the hall. This was the room Evan had described in his absurd scenario of lonely bachelor sitting by the fire with his dog.

"Would you like some something cold to drink? Or perhaps coffee?"

"No, thank you," Mary Jo answered. She chose the dark green leather wing chair angled in front of the fireplace. Mrs. Dryden sat in its twin.

"I realize you were surprised to see me with Evan yesterday."

"Yes," Lois agreed, her hands primly folded in her lap, "but who my son chooses to date is really none of my concern."

"That's very diplomatic of you. But I suspect you'd rather Evan dated someone other than me."

"Mary Jo, please. I feel we got started on the wrong foot all those years ago. It was entirely my fault, and I've wished many times since that I'd been more thoughtful. I have the feeling I deeply offended you and, my dear girl, that wasn't my intention."

"I'm willing to put the past behind us," Mary Jo suggested, managing a small smile. "That was three years ago, and I was more than a little overwhelmed by your family's wealth and position. If there's anyone at fault, it was me."

"That's very gracious of you, my dear." Mrs. Dryden relaxed in her chair and demurely crossed her ankles.

"I love Evan," Mary Jo said, thinking it would be best to be as forthright as possible. "And I believe he loves me."

"I'm pleased for you both." No telltale emotion sounded in her voice. They could have been discussing the weather for all the feeling her words revealed.

"Evan has asked me to marry him," she announced, carefully watching the woman who sat across from her for any signs of disapproval.

"I'm very pleased." A small and all-too-brief smile accompanied her statement. "Have you set the date? I hope you two realize we'll need at least a year to plan the wedding. This type of event takes time and careful preparation."

"Evan and I have decided on a small, private ceremony."

"No," Lois returned adamantly. "That won't be possible."

"Why not?" Mary Jo asked, taken aback by the vehemence in the older woman's voice.

"My husband is a senator. The son of a man in my husband's position does not sneak away and get married in . . . in secret."

Mary Jo hadn't said anything about sneaking away or secrecy, but she wasn't there to argue. "I come from a large family, Mrs. Dryden. We—"

"There were ten of you or some such, as I recall." Her hands made a dismissive motion.

Mary Jo bristled. The woman made her parents sound as if they'd produced a warren of rabbits, instead of a large, happy family.

"My point," Mary Jo said, controlling her irritation with some difficulty, "is that neither my parents nor I could afford a big, expensive wedding."

"Of course," Lois said, sounding relieved. "We wouldn't expect your relatives to assume the cost of such an elaborate affair. Walter and I would be more than happy to foot the bill."

"I appreciate the offer, and I'm sure my parents would, too, but I'm afraid we could never accept your generosity. Tradition says that the bride's family assumes the cost of the wedding, and my father is a very traditional man.''

"I see." Mrs. Dryden gnawed her lower lip. "There must be some way around his pride. Men can be such sticklers over things like this." For the first time she sounded almost friendly. "I'll think of something. Just leave it to me."

"There's something you don't understand. An ostentatious wedding isn't what I want, either."

"But you must. I've already explained why it's necessary. We wouldn't want to create even a breath of scandal with some hushed-up affair. Why, that could do untold damage to my husband and to Evan's political future."

"Breath of *scandal?*"

"My dear girl, I don't mean to be rude, and please forgive me if I sound like an old busybody, but there are people who'd delight in finding the least little thing to use against Walter."

"But I'm marrying Evan, not Walter."

"I realize that. But you don't seem to understand that these matters have to be handled...delicately. We must start planning immediately. The moment the announcement is made, you and your family will be the focus of media attention."

Mary Jo's head started to spin. "I'm sure you're mistaken. Why should anyone care about me or my family?"

Lois had begun wringing her hands. "I don't suppose it does any harm to mention it, although I must ask you not to spread this information around. Walter has been contacted by a longtime friend who intends to enter the presidential campaign this coming year. This friend has tentatively requested Walter to be his running mate, should he garner the party's nomination.''

Mary Jo developed an instant throbbing headache.

"My husband and I must avoid any situation that might put him in an unflattering light.''

"We could delay the wedding.'' She'd been joking, but Evan's mother looked greatly relieved.

"Would you?'' she asked hopefully.

"I'll talk to Evan.''

At the mention of her youngest son, Lois Dryden frowned. "Shouldn't he be here with you? It seems a bit odd that you'd tell me about your engagement without him.''

"I wanted the two of us to chat first,'' Mary Jo explained.

"An excellent idea,'' Lois said with a distinct nod of her head. "Men can be so difficult. If you and I can agree on certain...concerns before we talk to Evan and my husband, I feel sure we can work everything out to our mutual satisfaction.''

"Mrs. Dryden, I'm a kindergarten teacher. I think you should know I feel uncomfortable with the idea of becoming a media figure.''

"I'll do whatever I can to help you, Mary Jo. I realize it's a lot to have thrust on you all at once, but if you're going to marry my son, you have to learn how to handle the press. I'll teach you how to use them to your advantage and how to turn something negative into a positive.''

Mary Jo's headache increased a hundredfold. "I don't think I've been clear enough, Mrs. Dryden. I'm more than uncomfortable with this—I refuse to become involved in it."

"Refuse?" She repeated the word as if unsure of the meaning.

"I've already explained my feelings to Evan," Mary Jo continued. "I love your son so much…" Her voice shook and she stopped speaking for a moment. "I'm not like you or your husband, or Evan for, that matter. Nor do I intend to be. When Evan asked me to marry him, I told him all this."

A frown creased Lois Dryden's brow. "I'm not sure I understand."

"Perhaps I'm not explaining it right. Basically, I refuse to live my life seeking the approval of others. I want a small, private wedding and Evan has agreed."

"But what about the future, when Evan decides to enter politics? Trust me, Mary Jo, the wife's position is as demanding as that of her husband."

"I'm sure that's true. But I'd hate the kind of life you're describing. Evan knows that and understands. He's also agreed that as long as I feel this way, he won't enter politics."

His mother vaulted out of her chair. "But you can't do this! Politics is Evan's destiny. Why, from the time he was in grade school his teachers have told me what a natural leader he is. He was student-body president in high school *and* in college. From his early twenties on, he's been groomed for this very thing. I can well visualize my son in the White House someday."

His mother had lofty plans indeed. "Is this what Evan wants?"

"Of course it is," she said vehemently. "Ask him yourself. His father and brother have had countless conversations with him about this. If my son were to marry a woman who didn't appreciate his abilities or understand his ambitions, it might ruin him.''

If the words had come from anyone other than Lois Dryden, Mary Jo would have thought them absurd and melodramatic. But this woman believed implicitly what she said.

''Evan's marrying the right kind of woman is crucial to your plans for his future, isn't it?'' Mary Jo asked with infinite sadness.

Mrs. Dryden looked decidedly uncomfortable. ''Yes.''

''I'm not that woman.''

The older woman sighed. ''I realize that. The question is, what do you intend to do about it?''

CHAPTER EIGHT

"I LOVE EVAN," Mary Jo insisted again, but even as she spoke, she realized that loving him wasn't enough. Although she'd matured and wasn't the skittish, frightened woman she'd been three years earlier, nothing had really changed. If she married Evan, she might ruin his promising career. It was a heavy burden to carry.

Mary Jo couldn't change who and what she was; nor should she expect Evan to make all the concessions, giving up his future.

"I'm sure you do love my son," Lois said sincerely.

"And he loves me," Mary Jo added, keeping her back straight and her head high. She angled her chin at a proud, if somewhat defiant, tilt, unwilling to accept defeat. "We'll work this out somehow," she said confidently. "There isn't anything two people who love each other can't resolve. We'll find a way."

"I'm sure you will, my dear." Lois Dryden's mouth formed a sad smile that contradicted her reassurances. "In any case, you're perfectly right. You should discuss this all with Evan and reach a decision together."

The older woman smoothed an invisible wrinkle from her dove-gray skirt. "Despite what you may think, Mary Jo, I have no personal objections to your marrying my son. When the two of you separated some time ago, I wondered if it had something to do with our little talk. I don't mind telling you I suffered more than a few regrets. I never intended to hurt you, and if I did, I beg your forgiveness."

"You certainly opened my eyes," Mary Jo admitted. Evan's mother had refined that talent over the past few years, she noted silently.

"I might sound like a interfering old woman, but I do hope you'll take our little talk to heart. I trust you'll seriously consider what we've discussed." She sighed. "I love Evan, too. God has blessed me with a very special family, and all I want is what's best for my children. I'm sure your parents feel the same way about you."

"They do." The conversation was becoming more and more unbearable. Mary Jo wanted desperately to leave. And she needed to talk to Evan, to share her concerns and address their future. But deep down she'd caught a fearful glimpse of the truth.

Mary Jo stood up abruptly and offered Mrs. Dryden her hand. "Thank you for your honesty and your insights. It wasn't what I wanted to hear, but I suppose it's what I needed to know. I'm sure this was just as difficult for you. We have something in common, Mrs. Dryden. We both love your son. Evan wouldn't be the man he is without your love and care. You have a right to be proud."

Evan's mother took Mary Jo's hand in both of her own and held it firmly for several moments. "I appreciate that. Do keep in touch, won't you?"

Mary Jo nodded. "If you wish."

The older woman led her to the front door and walked out to the circular driveway with her. Mary Jo climbed into her car and started the engine. As she pulled away, she glanced in her rearview mirror to find Lois Dryden's look both thoughtful and troubled.

Normally Mary Jo joined her family for their Sunday get-togethers. But not this week. Needing time and privacy to sort out her thoughts, she drove to the marina. She parked, then walked slowly to the waterfront. The wind coming off the ocean was fresh and tangy with salt. She had to think, and what better place than here, where she'd spent countless happy hours in Evan's company?

How long she sat on the bench overlooking the water she didn't know. Time seemed to be of little consequence. She gazed at the boats moving in and out of their narrow passageways. The day had turned cloudy, which suited her somber mood.

Standing, she walked along the pier, once again reviewing her conversation with Evan's mother. Her steps slowed as she realized no amount of brooding would solve the problems. She needed to talk to Evan, and soon, before she lost her nerve.

She found a pay phone, plunked in a quarter and dialed his home number.

"Mary Jo. Thank goodness! Where were you?" Evan asked. "I've been calling your place every fifteen minutes. I have some wonderful news."

"I... had an errand to run," she said, not wanting to elaborate just then. He sounded terribly excited. "What's your good news?"

"I'll tell you the minute I see you."

"Do you want to meet somewhere?" she asked.

"How about Rowe's Wharf? We can take a stroll along the pier. If you want, we can visit the aquarium. I haven't been there in years. When we're hungry we can find a seafood restaurant and catch a bite to eat." He paused and laughed at his own sorry joke. "No pun intended."

"That'll be great," she said, finding it difficult to rouse the proper enthusiasm.

"Mary Jo?" His voice rose slightly. "What's wrong? You sound upset."

"We need to talk."

"All right," he agreed guardedly. "Do you want me to pick you up?" When she declined, he said, "I'll meet you there in half an hour, okay?"

"Okay." It was ironic, Mary Jo mused, that Evan could be so happy while she felt as if her entire world was about to shatter.

When she finished speaking to Evan, Mary Jo phoned her mother and told her she wouldn't be joining them for dinner. Marianna knew instantly that something wasn't right, but Mary Jo promised to explain later.

From the marina she drove down Atlantic Avenue and found a suitable place to park. It had been less than twenty-four hours, and already she was starved for the sight of Evan. It seemed unthinkable to live the rest of her life without him.

He was standing on the wharf waiting for her when she arrived. His face lighted up as she approached, and he held out both hands to her.

Mary Jo experienced an immediate sense of comfort the moment their fingers touched. In another second, she was securely wrapped in his arms. He held her against him as though he didn't intend to ever let her go. And she wished she didn't have to leave the protective shelter of his arms.

"I've missed you," he breathed against her temple. "Lord, how I've missed you." He threaded his fingers lovingly through her windblown hair.

"We spent nearly all of yesterday together," she reminded him lightly, although she shared his feelings. Even a few hours apart left her wondering how she'd managed to survive all those years without him. How she'd ever do it again...

"I love you, Mary Jo. Don't forget that."

"I won't." Loving him as she did, she found his words an intense comfort. She buried her face in his neck and clung to him, wanting to believe with everything she possessed that there was a way for them to find happiness together.

"Now tell me your good news," she murmured. Evan eased her out of his arms, but tucked her hand inside his elbow and pressed it there. His eyes were shining with excitement.

"Damian and I had a long talk last evening," Evan said. "I phoned to tell him about the two of us, and he's absolutely delighted. Jessica, too. They both send their congratulations by the way."

"Thank them for me," she said softly. "So come on, tell me your news." She leaned against him as they strolled leisurely down the wharf.

"All right, all right. Damian's been in contact with a number of key people over the past few weeks. The general consensus is that the time for me to make my move into the political arena is now."

Mary Jo felt as though a fist had been plowed into her midsection. For a moment she remained frozen. She couldn't breathe. Couldn't think. She was dimly aware of Evan beside her, still talking.

"Now?" she broke in. "But I thought...you said..."

"I know it probably seems way too early to be discussing next year's elections," Evan went on to say, his face alive with energy. "But we've got some catching up to do. I won't file for office until after the first of the year, but there're a million things that need to be done before then."

"What office do you intend to run for?" Her mind was awhirl with doubts and questions. The sick feeling in the pit of her stomach refused to go away. She felt both cold and feverishly hot at the same time.

"I'm running for city council. There's nothing I'd enjoy more. And, Mary Jo," he said with a broad grin, "I know I can make a difference in our city. I have so many ideas and I've got lots of time, and I don't mind working hard." He raised her hand to his lips and kissed the knuckles. "That's one of the reasons I want us to be married as soon as it can be arranged. We'll work together, side by side, the way my father and mother did when he ran for the Senate."

"I—"

"You'll need to quit your teaching job."

So many objections rose up in her she didn't know which one to address first. "Why can't I teach?"

He looked at her as if the question surprised him. "You don't have to work anymore, and besides, I'm going to need you. Don't you see, sweetheart? This is just the beginning. There's a whole new life waiting for the two of us.''

''Have you talked this over with your parents?'' Mrs. Dryden must have already known, Mary Jo mused.

''Dad and I discussed it this morning, and he agrees with Damian. The timing is right. Naturally, he'd like to see me run for mayor a few years down the road, and I might, but there's no need to get ahead of ourselves. I haven't been elected to city council yet.''

''What did your mother have to say?''

''I don't know if Dad's had the chance to talk to her yet. What makes you ask?''

''I . . . visited her this morning,'' Mary Jo admitted, studying the water. It was safer to look out over Boston Harbor than at the man she loved.

''You spent the morning with my mother?'' Evan stopped. ''At Whispering Willows?''

''Yes.''

His eyebrows shot straight toward his hairline. ''Why would you go and visit my mother?''

Mary Jo heaved in a deep breath and held it until her chest ached. ''There's something you should know, Evan. Something I should have told you a long time ago.'' She hesitated, finding it difficult to continue. When she did, her voice was low and strained. ''When I broke our engagement three years ago, it wasn't because I'd fallen in love with another man. There was never anyone else. It was all a big lie.''

She felt him stiffen. He frowned and his eyes narrowed, first with denial and then with disbelief. He shook off her hand and she walked over to the pier, waiting for him to join her.

It took him several moments.

"I'm not proud of that lie," she told him, "and I apologize for stooping to such cowardly methods. You deserved far better, but I wasn't strong enough or mature enough to confront you with the truth."

"Which was?" He was obviously making a strenuous effort to keep his voice level and dispassionate. But his fists were clenched. She could feel his anger, had anticipated it, understood it.

"Various reasons," she confessed. "I invented another love interest because I knew you'd believe me, and...and it avoided the inevitable arguments. I couldn't have dealt with a long-drawn-out debate."

"That makes no sense whatsoever." He sounded angry now, and Mary Jo couldn't blame him. "You'd better start at the beginning," he suggested after a long silence, gather his resolve. "What was it we would have argued about?"

"Our getting married."

"Okay," he said, obviously still not understanding.

"It all started the evening you took me to meet your family," Mary Jo began. "I'd realized you were wealthy, of course, but I had no idea how prominent your family was. I was naive and inexperienced, and when your mother asked me some...pertinent questions, I realized a marriage between us wouldn't work."

"What kind of 'pertinent' questions?" The words were stiff with contained fury.

"Evan, please, it doesn't matter."

"The hell it doesn't!"

Mary Jo briefly closed her eyes. "About my family and my background, and how suitable I'd be as a political wife. She stressed the importance of your marrying the right woman."

"It appears my mother and I need to have a chat."

"Don't be angry, Evan. She wasn't rude or cruel, but she brought up a few truths I hadn't faced. Afterward, I was convinced a marriage between us would never survive. We have so little in common. Our backgrounds are nothing alike, and I was afraid that in time you'd... you'd regret having married me."

He made a disgusted sound. "And so you made up this ridiculous lie and walked out of my life, leaving me lost and confused and so shaken it..." He paused as if he'd said more than he'd intended.

"I behaved stupidly—I know that. But I hurt, too, Evan. Don't think it was easy on me. I suffered. Because I loved you then and I love you still."

He sighed heavily. "I appreciate your honesty, Mary Jo, but let's put the whole mess behind us. It doesn't concern us anymore. We're together now and will be for the next fifty years. That's all that matters."

Tears blurred Mary Jo's eyes as she watched the airport shuttle boat cruise across Boston Harbor. The waters churned and foamed—like her emotions, she thought irrelevantly.

"It's quite apparent, however," Evan continued, "that I need to have a heart-to-heart with my dear, sweet, interfering mother."

"Evan, she isn't the one to blame. Breaking up, lying to you—that was *my* bad idea. But it isn't going to happen again."

"I won't let you out of my life that easily a second time."

"I don't plan on leaving," she whispered. He placed his arm around her shoulder, and Mary Jo slid her own arm around his waist. For a moment they were content in the simple pleasure of being together.

"Because of that first meeting with your mother, I felt it was important to talk to her again," Mary Jo said, wanting to explain why she'd gone to see Mrs. Dryden that morning. "She's a wonderful woman, Evan, and she loves you very much."

"Fine. But I refuse to allow her to interfere in our lives. If she doesn't understand that now, she will when I finish talking to her."

"Evan, please! She did nothing more than open my eyes to a few home truths."

"What did she have to say this morning?"

"Well...she had some of the same questions as before."

"Such as?" he demanded.

"You want us to be married soon, right?"

He nodded. "The sooner the better." Bending his head, he kissed a corner of her mouth. "As I said earlier, we have three years of lost time to make up for. Keep that house with all those empty bedrooms in mind."

Despite the ache in her heart, Mary Jo smiled. "Your mother told me that a small, private wedding might cause problems for your father."

"Whose wedding is this?" Evan cried. "We'll do this our way, sweetheart. Don't worry about it."

"It could be important, Evan," she countered swiftly. "Your father can't be associated with anything that . . . that could be misinterpreted."

Evan laughed outright. "In other words, she prefers to throw a large, gala wedding with a cast of thousands? That's ridiculous."

"I . . . think she might be right."

"That's the kind of wedding you want?" Evan asked, his eyes revealing his disbelief.

"No. It isn't what I want at all. But on the other hand, I wouldn't want to do anything to hurt your father."

"Trust me, sweetheart, you won't." He gave her an affectionate squeeze. "Now you listen. We're going to be married and we'll have the kind of wedding *we* want, and Mother won't have any choice but to accept it."

"But, Evan, what if our rushed wedding did cause speculation?"

"What if it did? Do you think I care? Or my father, either, for that matter? My mother is often guilty of making mountains out of molehills. She loves to worry. In this day and age, it's ridiculous to stew about such things."

"But—"

He silenced her with a kiss thorough enough to leave her feeling certain anything was possible. "I love you, Mary Jo. If it was up to me, we'd take the next plane to Las Vegas and be married this evening."

"People might gossip." She managed to dredge up one last argument.

"Good. The more my name's in circulation, the better."

Mary Jo's spirits had lightened considerably. She so desperately wanted to believe him she didn't stop to question what he was saying.

"It's settled, then. We'll be married as soon as we can make the arrangements. Mom can make all the fuss she wants, but it isn't going to do her any good."

"I . . . There are some other things we need to talk over first."

"There are?" He sounded exasperated.

She leaned against the pier, knotting and unknotting her hands. "You're excited about running for city council, aren't you?"

"Yes," he admitted readily. "This is something I want, and I'm willing to work for it. I wouldn't run for office if I wasn't convinced I could make some positive changes. This is exactly the right way for me to enter politics, especially while Dad's in the Senate."

She turned to study him. "What if I asked you not to run?"

Evan took several moments to mull over her words. "Why would you do that?"

"What if I did?" she asked again. "What would you do then?"

"First, I'd need to know exactly what you objected to."

"What if I reminded you I wasn't comfortable in the spotlight? Which, I might add, was something we discussed just yesterday. I'm not the kind of person who's comfortable living my life in a fishbowl."

"It wouldn't be like that," he protested.

Her smile was sad. Evan didn't understand. He'd grown up accustomed to having people interested in his personal life. Even now, his dating habits often enough provided speculation for the society pages.

"It *would* be like that, Evan. Don't kid yourself."

"Then you'll adjust," he said with supreme confidence.

"I'll adjust," she repeated slowly. "What if I don't? Then what happens? I could be an embarrassment to you. My family might be as well. Let me give you an example. Just recently, Jack and Rich were so upset over this investment problem my father's having that they were ready to go to Adison's office and punch him out. If we hadn't stopped them, they'd have been thrown in jail. The press would have a field day with that."

"You're overreacting."

"Maybe," she agreed grudgingly, then added with emphasis, "but I don't think so. I told you before how I feel about this. You didn't believe me, did you? You seem to think a pat on the head and a few reassurances are all I need. You've discounted everything I've said to you."

"Mary Jo, please—"

"In case you haven't noticed, I—I have this terrible habit of blushing whenever I'm the center of attention. I'm not the kind of woman your mother is. She enjoys the spotlight, loves arranging social events. She has a gift for making everyone feel comfortable and welcome. I can't do that, Evan. I'd be miserable."

Evan said nothing, but his mouth tightened.

"You may think I'm being selfish and uncaring, but that isn't true. I'm just not the right woman for you."

"Because my mother said so."

"No, because of who and what I am."

Evan sighed heavily. "I can see that you've already got this all worked out."

"Another thing. I'm a good teacher and I enjoy my job. I'd want to continue with my kindergarten class after we were married."

Evan took several steps away from her and rubbed his hand along the back of his neck. "Then there's nothing left for me to say, is there? I'll talk to Damian and explain that everything's off. I won't run for city council, not if it makes you that uncomfortable."

"Oh, Evan." She was on the verge of tears. This was exactly what she'd feared. Exactly what she didn't want. "Don't you see?" she pleaded, swallowing back a sob. "I can't marry you knowing I'm holding you back from your dreams. You may love me now, but in time you'd grow to resent me, and it would ruin our marriage."

"You're more important to me than any political office," Evan said sharply. "You're right, Mary Jo, you did tell me how you felt about getting involved in politics, and I did discount what you said. I grew up in a family that was often in the limelight. This whole thing is old hat to me. I was wrong not to have considered your feelings."

She closed her eyes in an effort to blot out his willingness to sacrifice himself. "It just isn't going to work, Evan. In the beginning you wouldn't mind, but later it would destroy us. It would hurt your family, too. This isn't only your dream, it's theirs."

"Leave my family to me."

"No. You're a part of them and they're a part of you. Politics has been your dream from the time you were a boy. You told me yourself that you believe you can make a difference to the city's future."

By now, the tears were running down her face. Impatiently she brushed them aside and forced herself to continue. "How many times are you going to make me say it? *I'm not the right woman for you.*"

"You *are* the right woman," he returned forcefully. His hands gripped her shoulders and he pulled her toward him, his eyes fierce and demanding. "I'm not listening to any more of this. We've loved each other too long. We're meant to be together."

Mary Jo closed her eyes again and hung her head. "There's someone else out there—from the right family, with the right background. A woman who'll share your ambition and your dreams, who'll work with you and not against you. A woman who'll...love you, too."

"I can't believe you're saying this." His grip tightened on her shoulder until it was almost painful, but she knew he didn't even realize it. "It's you I love. It's you I want to marry."

Mary Jo sadly shook her head.

"If you honestly believe there's another woman for me, why didn't I fall in love with someone else? I had three whole years to find this phantom woman you mention. Why didn't I?"

"Because your eyes were closed. Because you were too wrapped up in your own pain to look. For whatever reasons . . . I don't know . . ."

"Is this what you want? To walk out of my life a second time as if we meant nothing to each other?" He was beginning to attract attention from passersby, and he lowered his voice.

"No," she admitted. "This is killing me. I'd give anything to be the kind of woman you need, but I can only be me. If I ask you to accept who I am, then . . . I can't ask you to be something you're not."

"Don't do this," he said between clenched teeth. "We'll find a way."

How she wanted to believe that. How she wished it could be possible.

Evan drew a deep breath and released her shoulder. "Let's not make any drastic decisions now. We're both emotionally spent. Nothing has to be determined right this minute." He paused and gulped another deep breath. "Let's sleep on it and we can talk in the morning. All right?"

Mary Jo nodded. She couldn't have endured much more of this.

THE FOLLOWING MORNING Evan phoned the office shortly after she'd arrived and told her he'd be in late. His voice was cool, without a hint of emotion, as he asked her to reschedule his first two appointments.

Mary Jo thought she might as well have been speaking to a stranger. She longed to ask him how he was or if he'd had any further thoughts, but it was clear he wanted to avoid speaking to her about anything personal.

With a heavy heart, she began her morning duties. Around nine-thirty, the office door opened and Damian walked in. He paused as if he wasn't sure he'd come to the right room.

"Evan won't be in until eleven this morning," she explained.

"Yes, I know." For a man she'd assumed was utterly confident, Damian appeared doubtful and rather hesitant. "It wasn't Evan I came to see. It was you."

"Me?" She looked up at Damian, finding his gaze warm and sympathetic. "Why?"

"Evan stopped by the house yesterday afternoon to talk to both Jessica and me. He was confused and..."

"Hurt," Mary Jo supplied for him. She knew exactly what Evan was feeling because she'd felt the same way.

"I don't know that my talking to you will solve anything, but I thought I should give it a try. I'm not sure my brother would appreciate my butting into his personal business, but he did it once for me. I figure I owe him one." Damian's smile was fleeting. "I don't know if this is what you want to hear, but Evan sincerely loves you."

A lump developed in her throat and she nodded. "I realize that." She sincerely loved him, too.

"From what Evan said to us, I gather he's decided against running for city council. He also told us why he felt he had to back out. Naturally, I support any decision he chooses to make."

"But..." There had to be a "but" in all this.

"But it would be a shame if he declined."

"I'm not going to let that happen," Mary Jo said calmly. "You see, I love Evan and I want what's best for him, and to put it simply, that isn't me."

"He doesn't believe that, Mary Jo, and neither do I."

She could see no reason to discuss the issue. "Where's he now?" she asked softly.

"He went to talk to our parents."

Their parents. If anyone could get him to face the truth, it was Lois Dryden. Mary Jo had approached the woman, strong and certain of her love, and walked away convinced she'd been living in a dreamworld. Lois Dryden was capable of opening Evan's eyes as no one else could.

"We both need time to think this through," Mary Jo murmured. "I appreciate your coming to me, Damian, more than I can say. I know you did it out of love, but what happens between Evan and me, well, that's our concern."

"You didn't ask for my advice, but I'm going to give it to you, anyway," Damian said. "Don't be so quick to give up."

"I won't," she promised.

Mary Jo was sitting at her desk sorting mail when Evan arrived shortly after eleven. She stood up to greet him, but he glanced past her and said tonelessly, "I can't fight both of you." Then he walked into his office and closed the door.

His action said more than his words. In her heart, Mary Jo had dared to hope that if Evan confronted his parents and came away with his convictions intact, there might be a chance for them.

But obviously that hadn't happened. One look plainly revealed his resignation and regret. He'd accepted from his parents what he wouldn't from her. The truth.

Sitting back down, Mary Jo typed out her letter of resignation and signed it. Next she phoned a temporary employment agency and made the arrangements for her replacement to arrive that afternoon.

When she'd finished, she tapped lightly on his closed door and let herself into his office.

"Yes?" Evan said.

She found him standing in front of the window, hands clasped behind his back. After a moment, he turned to face her.

With tears blocking her throat, she laid the single sheet on his desk and crossed to stand beside him.

His gaze went from the letter to her and back. "What's that?"

"My letter of resignation. My replacement will be here within the hour. I'll finish out the day—show her around and explain her duties."

She half expected him to offer a token argument, but he said nothing. She pressed her hand against the side of his face and smiled up at him. His features blurred as the tears filled her eyes.

"Goodbye, Evan," she whispered.

CHAPTER NINE

A WEEK PASSED and the days bled into one another until Mary Jo couldn't distinguish morning from afternoon. A thousand regrets hounded her at all times of the day and night.

Blessed with a loving family, Mary Jo accepted their comfort, needed it. There was for all of them, some consolation in the news that came from Evan. Through his new secretary, he'd been in touch with her father regarding Adison Investments.

Mary Jo heard from him, too. Once. In a brief letter explaining that Adison would be forthcoming with the return of the original investment money, plus interest. Since he'd calculated his fee for an extended lawsuit, she owed him nothing.

Mary Jo read the letter several times, looking for a message. Anything. But there were only three short sentences, their tone crisp and businesslike, with no hidden meaning that she could decipher. Tears blurred her eyes as she lovingly ran her finger over his signature. She missed him terribly, felt empty and lost and this was as close as she would ever be to him again— her finger caressing his signature at the end of a letter.

Another week passed. Mary Jo was no less miserable than she'd been the first day after she'd stopped working for Evan. She knew it would take time and effort to accept the infeasibility of her love for him, but she wasn't ready. Not yet. So she stayed holed up in her apartment, listless and heartbroken.

The fact that the summer days were glorious—all sunshine and blue sky—didn't help. The least Mother Nature could have done was cooperate and match her mood with dark gray clouds and gloomy days.

She dragged herself out of bed late that morning and didn't bother to eat until early afternoon. Now she sat in front of the television dressed in her nightie and munching dry cornflakes. She hadn't been to the grocery store in weeks and had long since run out of milk. And just about everything else.

The doorbell chimed, and Mary Jo shot an accusing glance in the direction of her front door. It was probably her mother or one of her sisters-in-law, who seemed to think it was up to them to boost her spirits. So they invented a number of ridiculous excuses to pop in unexpectedly.

The love and support of her family was important, but all Mary Jo wanted at the moment was to be left alone. To eat her cornflakes in peace.

She set the bowl aside, walked over to the door and squinted through the peephole. She caught a glimpse of a designer purse, but unfortunately whoever was holding it stood just outside her view.

"Who is it?" she called out.

"Jessica."

Mary Jo pressed her forehead against the door and groaned. She was an emotional and physical wreck. The last person she wanted to see was anyone related to Evan.

"Mary Jo, please open the door," Jessica called. "We need to talk. It's about Evan."

Nothing could have been more effective. Mary Jo didn't want company. She didn't want to talk. But the minute Jessica said Evan's name, she turned the lock and opened the door. Standing in the doorway, she closed her eyes against the painfully bright sun.

"How are you?" Jessica asked, walking right in.

"About as bad as I look," Mary Jo mumbled, shutting the door behind her. "What about Evan?"

"Same as you." She strode into the room, removed a stack of papers from the rocking chair and planted herself on it as if she intended to stay for a while.

"Where's Andy?" Mary Jo asked, still holding the doorknob.

Jessica crossed her legs, rocking gently as if she had all the time in the world. "My mother has him—for the *day*."

Mary Jo noted the emphasis. Jessica intended to stay here until she got what she wanted.

"I told Mom I had a doctor's appointment, and I do—later," Jessica continued. "I think I'm pregnant again." A radiant happiness shone from her eyes.

"Congratulations." Although Mary Jo was miserable, she was pleased for her friend, who was clearly delighted.

"I know it's none of my business," Jessica said sympathetically, "but tell me what happened between you and Evan."

"I'm sure he's already explained." Mary Jo wasn't up to hauling up all the painful details. Besides, it would solve nothing.

Jessica laughed shortly. "Evan talk? You've got to be joking. He wouldn't say so much as a word. Both Damian and I've tried to get him to discuss what happened, but it hasn't done a bit of good."

"So you've come to me."

"Exactly." Jessica was obviously determined to stay until she learned what she wanted to know.

"Please don't do this, Jessica," Mary Jo said, fighting back the tears. "It's just too painful."

"But you both love each other so much."

"That's why our breakup's necessary. It isn't easy on either of us, but this is the way it has to be."

Jessica tossed her hands in the air. "You're a pair of fools. There's no talking to Evan, and you're not much better. What's it going to take to get you two back together?"

"A miracle," Mary Jo answered.

Jessica took several moments to digest this. "Is there anything I can do?"

"No," Mary Jo said sadly. There wasn't anything anyone could do. But one thing was certain: she couldn't continue like this. Sliding from one day to the next without a thought to the future. Buried in the pain of the past, barely able to live in the present.

"You're sure?"

"I'm thinking of leaving Boston," she said suddenly. The impulse had come unexpectedly, and in a heartbeat Mary Jo knew it was the right thing to do. She couldn't live in this town, this state, without constantly being bombarded with information about the Dryden family. Not a week passed that his father wasn't in the news for one reason or another, or so it seemed. It wouldn't get any better once Evan was elected to city council.

Escape seemed her only answer.

"Where would you go?" Jessica pressed.

Anywhere that wasn't here. "The Northwest," she said again, blurting out the first destination that came to mind. "Washington, maybe Oregon. I've heard that part of the country's beautiful." Teachers were needed everywhere and she shouldn't have much trouble obtaining a position.

"So far away?" Jessica seemed to breathe the question.

The farther the better. Her family would argue with her, but for the first time in two weeks, Mary Jo had found a reason to look ahead.

Her parents would tell her she was running away, and Mary Jo would agree, but sometimes running was necessary. She remembered her father's talks with her older brothers; he'd explained that there might come a day when they'd find themselves in a no-win situation. The best thing to do, he'd told them, was to walk away. Surely this was one of those times.

"Thank you for coming," Mary Jo said, looking solemnly at her friend. "I appreciate it. Please let me know when the baby's born."

"I will," Jessica said, her eyes sad.

"I'll have my mother send me the results of the election next year. My heart will be with Evan."

It would always be with him.

Jessica left soon afterward, flustered and discouraged. They hugged and, amid promises to keep in touch, reluctantly parted. Mary Jo counted Evan's sister-in-law as a good friend.

Mary Jo was suddenly filled with purpose. She dressed, made a number of phone calls, opened the door and let the sunshine pour in. By late afternoon, she'd accomplished more than she had in the entire previous two weeks. Telling her parents her decision wouldn't be easy, but her mind was made up. It was now Tuesday. First thing next Monday morning, she was packing what she could in her car and heading west. As soon as she'd settled somewhere she'd send for her furniture.

Before Mary Jo could announce her decision, her father phoned her with the wonderful news that he'd received a cashier's check returning his investment. Not only that, Evan had put him in contact with a reputable financial adviser.

"That's great," Mary Jo said, blinking back tears. Hearing the relief in her father's voice was all the reward she would ever need. Although it had ultimately broken her heart, asking Evan to help her parents had been the right thing to do. Her father had gotten far more than his investment back. In the process he'd restored his pride and his faith in justice.

"I need to talk to you and Mom," Mary Jo announced, steeling herself for the inevitable confrontation. "I'll be over in a few minutes."

The meeting didn't go well. Mary Jo hadn't expected that it would. Her parents had a list of objections that lasted nearly an hour. Mary Jo's resolve didn't waver. She was leaving Boston; she would find a new life for herself.

To her surprise, her brothers sided with her. Jack insisted she was old enough to make her own decisions. His words did more to convince her parents than hours of her own arguments.

The Friday before she was leaving, Mary Jo spent the day with her mother. Marianna was pickling cucumbers in the kitchen, dabbing her eyes now and again when she didn't think Mary Jo was looking.

"I'm going to miss you," Marianna said, putting on a brave front.

Mary Jo's heart clenched. "I'll miss you, too. But, Mom, you make it sound like you'll never hear from me again. I promise to phone at least once a week."

"Call when the rates are cheaper, understand?"

Mary Jo suppressed a smile. "Of course."

"I talked to Evan," her mother mentioned casually as she was inserting large cloves of garlic into the sterilized canning jars.

Mary Jo froze, and her breath jammed in her chest.

"I told him you'd decided to leave Boston, and you know what he said?"

"No." The word rose from her throat on a bubble of hysteria.

"Evan said you'd know what was best." She paused as if carefully judging her words. "He didn't sound like himself. I'm worried about that boy, but I'm more concerned about you."

"Mom, I'm going to be fine."

"I know that. You're a Summerhill and we're strong people."

Mary Jo followed her mother, dropping a sprig of dill weed into each of the sparkling clean jars.

"You never told me what went wrong between you and Evan, not that you had to. I've got eyes and ears, and it didn't take much for me to figure out his family had something to do with all this."

Her mother's insight didn't come as any surprise, but Mary Jo neither confirmed nor denied it.

"The mail's here," Norman Summerhill said, strolling into the kitchen. "I had one of those fancy travel agencies send us a couple of brochures on the South Pacific. When you're finished packing those jars, let's sit down and read over what they've got to say."

Marianna's nod was eager. "We won't be long."

Her father set the rest of the mail on the table. The top envelope captured Mary Jo's attention. The return address was a bankruptcy court. She didn't think anything of it until later when her father opened the envelope.

"I wonder what this is?" he mumbled, sounding confused. He stretched his arms out in front of him to read it.

"Norman, for the love of heaven, get your glasses," Marianna chastised.

"I can see fine without them." He winked at Mary Jo. "Here, you read it for me." Mary Jo took the cover letter and scanned the contents. As she did, her stomach turned. The bankruptcy court had written her parents on behalf of Adison Investments. They were to complete the attached forms and list, with proof, the amount of their investment. Once all the documents were returned, the case would be heard.

The legal jargon was difficult for Mary Jo to understand, but one thing was clear. Adison Investments hadn't returned her father's money.

Evan had.

"It's nothing, Dad," Mary Jo said, not knowing what else to say.

"Then throw it away. I don't understand why we get so much junk mail these days. You'd think the environmentalists would do something about wasting all those trees."

Mary Jo stuck the envelope in her purse, made her excuses and left soon afterward. She wasn't sure what she was going to do, but if she didn't escape soon, there'd be no hiding her tears.

Evan had done this for her family because he loved her. This was his way of saying goodbye. Hot tears blurred her eyes, and sniffling, she rubbed the back of her hand across her face.

The blast of a car horn sounded from behind her and Mary Jo glanced in the direction of the noise. Adrenaline shot through her as she saw a full-size sedan barreling toward her.

The next thing she heard was metal slamming against metal. The sound exploded in her ears and she instinctively brought her hands up to her face. The impact was so strong she felt as though she were caught in the middle of an explosion.

Her world went into chaos. There was only pain. Her head started to spin, and her vision blurred. She screamed.

Her last thought before she lost consciousness was that she was going to die.

"WHY DIDN'T YOU CALL ME right away?" a gruff male voice demanded.

It seemed to come from a great distance away and drifted slowly toward Mary Jo as she floated, unconcerned, on a thick black cloud. It sounded like Evan's voice, but then again it didn't. The words came to her sluggish and slurred.

"We tried to contact you, but your secretary said you couldn't be reached."

The second voice belonged to her father, Mary Jo determined. But he, too, sounded odd, as if he were standing at the bottom of a deep well and yelling up at her. The words were distorted and they vibrated, making them difficult to understand. They seemed to take a very long time to reach her. Perhaps it was because her head hurt so badly. The throbbing was intense and painful.

"I came as soon as I heard." It was Evan again and he sounded sorry, as if he was to blame. "How seriously is she hurt?"

"Doc says she sustained a head injury. She's unconscious, but they claim she isn't in a coma."

"She'll wake up soon," her mother said in a soothing tone. "Now sit down and relax. Everything's going to be all right. I'm sure the doctor will be happy to answer any of your questions. Mary Jo's going to fine, just wait and see."

Her mother was comforting Evan as if he were one of her own children, Mary Jo realized. She didn't understand why Evan should be so worried. Perhaps he was afraid she was going to die. Perhaps she already had, but then she decided she couldn't be dead because she hurt too much.

"What have they done to her head?"

Mary Jo was anxious for that answer herself.

"They had to shave off her hair."

"Relax." It was her father speaking. "It'll grow back."

"It's just that she looks so..." Evan didn't finish the sentence.

"She'll be fine, Evan. Now sit down here by her side. I know it's a shock seeing her like this."

Mary Jo wanted to reassure Evan herself, but her mouth refused to open and she couldn't speak. Something must be wrong with her if she could hear but not see or speak. When she attempted to move, she found her arms and legs wouldn't cooperate. A sense of panic overwhelmed her and the pounding pain intensified.

Almost immediately she drifted away on the same dark cloud and the voices slowly faded. She longed to call out, to pull herself back, but she hadn't the strength. And this way, the pain wasn't nearly as bad.

THE NEXT THING Mary Jo heard was a soft thumping. It took her several moments to recognize what that particular sound meant. Someone was in her room, pacing. Whoever it was seemed impatient, or maybe anxious. She didn't know which.

"How is she?" A feminine voice that was vaguely familiar drifted soothingly toward Mary Jo. The pain in her head was back, and she desperately wanted it to go away.

"There's been no change." It was Evan who spoke. Evan was the one pacing her room. Knowing he was there filled her with a gentle sense of peace. She'd recover if Evan was with her. How she knew this, Mary Jo didn't question.

"How long have you been here?" The feminine voice belonged to Jessica, she decided.

"A few hours."

"It's more like twenty-four. I met Mary Jo's parents in the elevator. They're going home to get some sleep. You should, too. The hospital will call if there's any change."

"No."

Mary Jo laughed to herself. She'd recognize that stubborn streak of his anywhere.

"Evan," Jessica protested. "You're not thinking clearly."

"Yeah, I know. But I'm not leaving her, Jessica. You can argue if you want, but it won't do you a damn bit of good."

There was a short silence. Mary Jo heard a chair being dragged across the floor. It was coming toward her. "Mary Jo was leaving Boston, did you know?"

"I know," Evan returned. "Her mother called to tell me."

"Were you going to stop her?"

It took him a long time to answer. "No."

"But you love her."

"Jess, please, leave it alone."

Evan loved her and she loved him, and it was hopeless. A sob swelled within her chest and Mary Jo experienced an overwhelming urge to weep.

"She moved," Evan said sharply, excitedly. "Did you see it? Her hand flinched just now."

Mary Jo felt herself being pulled away once more into a black void where there was no sound. It seemed to close in around her like the folds of a dark, bulky blanket.

WHEN MARY JO OPENED her eyes, the first thing she saw was a patch of blue. It took her a moment to realize it was the sky from outside the hospital window. A scattering of clouds shimmied across the horizon. She blinked, trying to remember what she was doing in this bed, in this room.

She'd been in a car accident, that was it. She couldn't remember any details—except that she thought she was dying. Her head had hurt so badly. The throbbing wasn't nearly as intense now, but it was still there and the bright sunshine made her eyes water.

Rolling her head to the other side demanded a great deal of effort. Her mother was sitting at her bedside reading from a Bible and her father was standing on the other side of the room. He pressed his hands against the small of his back as if to relieve tired muscles.

"Mom." Mary Jo's voice was husky and low.

Marianna Summerhill vaulted to her feet. "Norman, Norman, Mary Jo's awake." Having said that, she covered her face with her hands and burst into tears.

It was very unusual to see her mother cry. Mary Jo looked at her father and saw that his eyes, too, were brimming with tears.

"So you decided to rejoin the living," her father said, raising her hand to his lips. "Welcome back."

Smiling required more strength than she had.

"How do you feel?" Her mother was dabbing at her eyes with a tissue and looking so pale that Mary Jo wondered if she'd been ill herself.

"Weird," she said hoarsely.

"The doctor said he expected you to wake up soon."

There was so much she wanted to ask, so much she had to say. "Evan?" she managed to croak.

"He was here," her mother answered. "From the moment he learned about the accident until just a few minutes ago. No one could convince him to leave."

"He's talking with some fancy specialist right now," her father explained. "I don't mind telling you, he's been beside himself with worry. We've all been scared."

Her eyes drifted shut. She felt so incredibly weak, and what energy she had evaporated quickly.

"Sleep," her mother cooed. "Everything's going to be fine."

No, no, Mary Jo protested, fighting sleep. Not yet. Not so soon. She had too many questions that needed answering. But the silence enveloped her once more.

It was night when she stirred again. The sky was dark and the heavens were flecked with stars. Moonlight softly illuminated the room.

She assumed she was alone, then noticed a shadowy figure against the wall. The still shape sat in the chair next to her bed. It was Evan, she realized, and he was asleep. His arms were braced against the edge of the mattress, supporting his head.

The comfort she felt in knowing he was with her was beyond measure. Reaching for his hand, she covered it with her own, then yawned and closed her eyes.

"ARE YOU HUNGRY?" Marianna asked, carrying in the hospital tray and setting it on the bedside table.

Mary Jo was sitting up for the first time. "I don't know," she said, surprised by how feeble her voice sounded.

"I talked to the doctor about the hospital menu," her mother said, giving her head a disparaging shake. "He assured me you'll survive on their cooking until I can get you home and feed you properly."

It probably wasn't all that amusing, but Mary Jo couldn't stop smiling. For the first time she really took note of her surroundings. The room was filled with fresh flowers. They covered every available surface; there were even half a dozen vases lined up on the floor.

"Who sent all the flowers?" she asked.

Her mother pointed toward the various floral arrangements. "Your brothers. Dad and I. Those two are from Jessica and Damian. Let me see—the teachers at your old school. Oh, the elaborate one is from the Drydens. That bouquet of pink carnations is from Gary."

"How sweet of everyone." But Mary Jo noticed that there were a number of bouquets her mother had skipped. Those, she strongly suspected, were from Evan.

Evan.

Just thinking about him made her feel so terribly sad. From the time she'd regained consciousness, he'd stopped coming to the hospital. He'd been there earlier, she was sure of it. The memories were too vivid not to be real. But as soon as she was out of danger, he'd left her life once more.

"Eat something," Marianna insisted. "I know it's not your mama's cooking, but it doesn't look too bad."

Mary Jo shook her head and leaned back against the pillow. "I'm not hungry."

"Sweetheart, please. The doctors won't let you come home until you've regained your strength."

Evan wasn't the only one with a stubborn streak. She folded her arms and refused to even look at the food. Eventually, she was persuaded to take a few bites, because it was clear her lack of appetite was distressing her mother.

When the tray was removed, Mary Jo slept. Her father was with her when she awoke. Her eyes met his, which were warm and tender.

"Was the accident my fault?" She had to know, she remembered so little of what had happened.

"No. The other car ran a red light."

"Was anyone else hurt?"

"No," he said, taking her hand in both of his.

"I'm sorry I worried you."

A slight smile crossed his face. "Your brothers were just as worried. And Evan."

"He was here, wasn't he?"

"Every minute. No one could get him to leave, not even his own family."

But he wasn't there now. When she really needed him.

Her father gently patted her hand, and when he spoke it was as if he'd been reading her thoughts. "Life has a way of making things right. Everything will turn out just the way it's supposed to. So don't you fret about Evan or his family or anything else. Just concentrate on getting well."

"I will." But her heart wasn't in it. Her heart was with Evan.

A WEEK PASSED, and Mary Jo regained more of her strength each day. With her head shaved, she looked as if she'd stepped out of a science-fiction movie. All she needed were the right clothes and a laser gun and she'd be real Hollywood material.

If she continued to improve at this pace, she should be discharged from the hospital within the next couple of days. That was good news—not that she didn't appreciate the excellent care she'd received.

Mary Jo spent part of the morning slowly walking the corridors in an effort to rebuild her strength. She still tired easily and took frequent breaks to chat with nurses and other patients. After a pleasant but exhausting couple of hours, she decided to go back to bed for a while.

As she entered her room, she stopped abruptly. Lois Dryden stood by the window, looking out of place in her tailored suit.

Lois must have sensed her return. There was no disguising her dismay when she saw Mary Jo's shaved, bandaged head. She seemed incapable of speech for a moment.

Mary Jo took the initiative. "Hello, Mrs. Dryden," she said evenly.

"Hello, my dear. I hope you don't mind my dropping in like this."

"No, of course I don't mind." Mary Jo made her way to the bed and got in, conscious of her still-awkward movements.

"I was very sorry to hear about your accident."

Mary Jo adjusted the covers around her legs and leaned back against the raised mattress. "I'm well on the way to recovery now."

"That's what I understand. I heard there's a possibility you'll be going home soon."

"I hope so."

"Is there anything I can do for you?"

The offer surprised Mary Jo. "No, but thank you."

Lois walked away from the window and stood at the foot of the bed, the picture of conventional propriety with her small hat and spotless white gloves. She looked directly at Mary Jo.

"I understand Jessica has come by a number of times," she said.

"Yes," Mary Jo answered. "She's been very kind. She brought me a tape player and some books on tape." Except that Mary Jo hadn't been able to concentrate on any of the stories. No sooner would the tape begin than she'd drift off to sleep.

"I suppose Jessica told you she and Damian are expecting again."

Without warning, Mary Jo's heart contracted painfully. "Yes, I'm delighted for them."

"Naturally, Walter and I are thrilled with the prospect of a second grandchild."

It became important not to look at Evan's mother, and Mary Jo focused her gaze out the window. The tightness in her chest refused to go away, and she realized the source of the pain was emotional. She longed for a child herself. Evan's child. They'd talked about their home, planned their family. The picture of the house he'd described, with a yard full of laughing, playing children flashed into her mind.

The house would never be built now. There would be no children. No marriage. No Evan.

"Of course, Damian is beside himself with happiness."

From somewhere deep inside, Mary Jo found the strength to say, "I imagine he is."

"There'll be a little less than two years between the two children. Andrew will be twenty months old by the time the baby's born."

Mary Jo wondered why Mrs. Dryden was telling her all this and could think of nothing more to say. She found the conversation exhausting. She briefly closed her eyes.

"I . . . I suppose I shouldn't tire you any longer."

"Thank you for stopping by," Mary Jo murmured politely.

Lois stepped toward the door, then hesitated and turned back to the bed. Mary Jo noticed that the older woman's hand trembled as she reached out and gripped the foot of the bed.

"Is something the matter?" Mary Jo asked, thinking perhaps she should ring for the nurse.

"Yes," Evan's mother said. "Something is very much the matter—and I'm the one at fault. You came to me not long ago because you wanted to marry my son. I discouraged you, and Evan, too, when he came to speak to his father and me."

"Mrs. Dryden, please—"

"No, let me finish." She took in a deep breath and leveled her gaze on Mary Jo. "Knowing what I do now, I would give everything I have if you'd agree to marry my son."

CHAPTER TEN

MARY JO WASN'T SURE she'd heard Evan's mother correctly. "I don't understand."

Instinctively, she knew that Mrs. Dryden was someone who rarely revealed her feelings. She knew that the older woman rarely lost control of a situation—or of herself. She seemed dangerously close to losing it now.

"Would...would you mind if I sat down?"

"Please do." Mary Jo wished she'd thought to suggest it herself.

Lois pulled the chair closer to the bed, and Mary Jo was surprised by how delicate, how fragile, she suddenly appeared. "Before I say anything more, I must ask your forgiveness."

"Mine?"

"Yes, my dear. When you came to me, happy and excited, to discuss marrying my son, I was impressed by your...your courage. Your sense of responsibility. You'd guessed my feelings correctly when Evan brought you to dinner three or so years ago. Although you were a delightful young woman, I couldn't picture you as his wife. My son, however, was clearly enthralled with you."

Mary Jo started to speak, but Mrs. Dryden shook her head, obviously determined to finish her confession. "I decided that very night that it was important for us to talk. I'd never intended to hurt you or Evan, and when I learned you were no longer seeing each other, I realized it might have had something to do with what I'd said to you."

"Mrs. Dryden, please, this isn't necessary."

"On the contrary. It's very necessary. If you're to be my daughter-in-law, and I sincerely hope you will be, then I feel it's vital for us to... to begin afresh."

Mary Jo's pulse began to hammer with excitement. "You meant what you said earlier, then? About wanting me to marry Evan?"

"Every word. Once we know each other a little better, you'll learn I rarely say what I don't mean. Now, please, allow me to continue."

"Of course. I'm sorry."

Mrs. Dryden gave her an ironic smile. "Once we're on more familiar terms, you won't need to be so apprehensive of me. I'm hoping we can be friends, Mary Jo. After all I pray you'll be the mother of my grandchildren." She smiled again. "Half of them, anyway."

Mary Jo blinked back her tears, deeply moved by the other woman's unmistakable contrition and by her generosity.

"Now... where was I?" Oh, yes, we were talking about three years ago. You and Evan had decided not to see each other again, and frankly—forgive me for this, Mary Jo—I was relieved. But Evan seemed to take the breakup very badly. I realized then that I might have acted too hastily. For months, I contemplated calling you myself. I'm ashamed to tell you I kept putting it off. No," she said and her voice shook, "I was a coward. I dreaded facing you."

"Mrs. Dryden, it was a long time ago."

"You're right, it was, but that doesn't lessen my guilt." She paused. "Evan changed that autumn. He'd always been such a lighthearted young man. He continued to joke and tease, but it wasn't the same. The happiness had gone out of his eyes. Nothing held his interest for long. He drifted from one brief relation-ship to another. He was miserable, and it showed."

In those bleak, lonely months, Mary Jo hadn't fared much better, but she said nothing about that now.

"It was during this time that Walter decided to run for the Senate, and our lives were turned upside down. Our one concern was Evan. The election was important to Walter, and in some ways, Evan was a problem. Walter discussed the situation with Evan... Oh, dear. None of this applies to the present situation. I'm getting sidetracked."

"No. Go on," Mary Jo pleaded.

"I have to admit I'm not proud of what we did. Walter and I felt strongly that Jessica Kellerman was the right woman for Evan, and we did what we could to encourage a relationship. As you know, Damian and Jessica fell in love. You'd think I'd have learned my lesson about interfering in my sons' lives, but apparently not."

Mary Jo wished she could say something to reassure Lois.

"Early this summer, Walter and I noticed a... new happiness in Evan. He seemed more like the way he used to be. Later we learned that you were working for him. I decided then and there that if you two decided to rekindle your romance, I'd do nothing to stand in your way."

"You didn't," Mary Jo said quickly.

"Then you came to me and insisted on a small, private wedding. It was obvious you didn't understand the social demands made upon a husband in politics. I could see you were getting discouraged, and I did nothing to change that. At the time it seemed for the best."

"Mrs. Dryden, you're taking on far more blame than you should."

"That's not all, Mary Jo." She clenched her purse with both gloved hands and hung her head. "Evan came to speak to Walter and me about the two of you. I don't believe I've ever seen him so angry. No other woman has ever held such power over my son. You see, Evan and I've always been close and it…pains me to admit this, but I was jealous. I told him that if you were willing to break off another engagement over the first disagreement, then you weren't the woman for him.

"I must have been more persuasive than I realized. Later Evan told me he couldn't fight both of us and that he'd decided to abide by your wishes."

"He said that to me, too," Mary Jo murmured.

"It's been several weeks now, but nothing's changed. My son still loves you very much. When you had this accident, he refused to leave the hospital. I came here myself early one morning and found Evan sitting alone in the hospital chapel." She paused and her lower lip trembled. "I knew then that you weren't some passing fancy in his life. He loves you as he's never loved another woman and probably won't again."

Mary Jo leaned forward. "I'll never be comfortable in the limelight, Mrs. Dryden," she said urgently. "But I'm willing to do whatever it takes to be the kind of wife Evan needs."

Mrs. Dryden snapped open her purse, took out a delicate white handkerchief and dabbed her eyes. "It's time for another confession, I'm afraid. I've always believed Evan would do well in politics. I've made no secret of my ambitions for my son, but that's what they were—*my* ambitions. Not his. If Evan does decide to pursue a political career, it should be his decision, not mine.

"In light of what's happened between you two, I'm determined to stay out of it entirely. Whatever happens now depends on Evan. On you, too, of course," she added hurriedly, "but I promise you, I won't interfere. I've finally learned my lesson."

Unable to speak, Mary Jo reached for the other woman's hand and held it tightly.

"I'd like it if we could be friends, Mary Jo," Lois added softly. "I'll do my damnedest to stop being an interfering old woman."

"My mother learned her lessons with my oldest brother, Jack, and his wife. You might like to speak to her sometime and swap stories," Mary Jo suggested.

"I'd like that." She stood and bent to kiss Mary Jo's cheek. "You'll go to Evan, then, when you're able?"

Mary Jo grinned. "As soon as I look a bit more presentable."

"You'll look wonderful to Evan now, believe me." The older woman touched her hand softly. "Make him happy, Mary Jo."

"I'll do my very best."

"And please let me know when your mother and I can talk. We have a million things to discuss about the wedding."

Mary Jo ventured, a little hesitantly, "The wedding will be small and private."

"Whatever you decide."

"But perhaps we could have a big reception afterward and invite the people you wouldn't want to offend by excluding."

"An excellent idea." Lois smiled broadly.

"Thank you for coming to see me."

A tear formed in the corner of one of Lois's eyes. "No. Thank *you,* my dear."

FROM THE DAY of Lois Dryden's visit, Mary Jo's recovery was little short of miraculous. She was discharged two days later and spent a week recuperating at her parents' home before she felt ready to confront Evan.

According to Jessica, he was frequently out on his sailboat. With her friend's help, it was a simple matter to discover when he'd scheduled an outing.

Saturday morning, the sun was bright and the wind brisk—a perfect sailing day. Mary Jo went down to the marina. Using Damian's key, she let herself in and climbed aboard Evan's boat to wait for him.

She hadn't been there long when he arrived. He must have seen her right away, although he gave no outward indication that he had.

She still felt somewhat uncomfortable about her hair, now about half an inch long. She'd tried to disguise it with a turban, but that only make her look as if she should be reading palms or tea leaves. So she left it unadorned.

"Mary Jo?"

"It hard to tell without the hair, right?" she joked.

"What are you doing here?" Evan wasn't unfriendly; nor did he seem particularly pleased to see her.

"I wanted to talk, and this is the place we do our best talking. Are you taking the boat out this morning?"

He ignored the question. "How are you?" The craft rocked gently as he climbed on deck and sat down beside her.

"Much better. A little weak, but I'm gaining more strength every day."

"When were you released from the hospital?"

Evan knew the answer as well as she did, Mary Jo was sure. Why was he making small talk at a time like this?

"You already know. Your mother told you, or Jessica." She paused. "You were at the hospital, Evan."

His mouth tightened, but he said nothing.

"There were periods when I could hear what was going on around me. I was awake, sort of, when you first got there. Another time, I heard you pacing my room, too, and I heard you again when Jessica came by once." She reached for Evan's hand and threaded her fingers through his. "One of the first times I actually woke was the middle of the night, and you were there, asleep."

"I've never been more frightened in my life," he said hoarsely, as if the words had been wrenched from his throat. He wrapped his arms around her then, but gently, with deliberate care. Mary Jo rested her head against his shoulder, and his grip on her tightened just a little. He buried his face in the delicate curve of her shoulder; she felt his warm strength. After a moment, he released her.

"I understand my parents' investment was returned to them—with interest," she said, her tone deceptively casual.

"Yes," he admitted. "They were among the fortunate few to have their money refunded."

"*Their* money?" She raised her hand to his mouth, kissing his knuckles. "Evan, I know what you did."

He frowned. He had that confused, what-are-you-talking-about expression down to an art.

"You might have been able to get away with it but, you see, the papers came."

"What papers?"

"The day of my accident my parents received a notice from the bankruptcy court—as I'm sure you know. If their investment had been returned, how do you explain that?"

He shrugged. "Don't have a clue."

"Evan, please, it's not necessary to play games with me."

He seemed to feel a sudden need to move around. He stood, stretched and moved to the far end of the sailboat. Pointedly, he glanced at his watch. "I wish I had time to chat, but unfortunately I'm meeting a friend."

"Evan, we need to talk."

"I'm sorry, but you should have let me know sooner. Perhaps we could get together some other time." He made an elaborate display of staring at the pier, then smiling and waving eagerly.

A tall, blond woman, incredibly slender and beautifully tanned, waved back. She had the figure of a fashion model and all but purred when Evan hopped out of the boat and met her dockside. She threw her arms around his neck and kissed him, bending one shapely leg at the knee.

Mary Jo was stunned. To hear his mother speak, Evan was a lost, lonely man, so in love with her that his world had fallen apart. Clearly, there was something Mrs. Dryden didn't know.

In her rush to climb out of the sailboat, Mary Jo nearly fell overboard. With her nearly bald head and the clothes that hung on her because of all the weight she'd lost, she felt like the little match girl standing barefoot in the snow. Especially beside this paragon of feminine perfection.

She suffered through an introduction that she didn't hear, made her excuses and promptly left. When she was back in her car, she slumped against the steering wheel, covering her face with both hands.

Shaken and angry, she returned her parents' place and called Jessica to tell her what had happened. She was grateful her parents were out.

She paced the living room in an excess of nervous energy until Jessica arrived, an hour later, looking flustered and disgruntled. "Sorry it took me so long, but I took a cab and it turned out to be the driver's first day on the job. We got lost twice. So what's going on? Lord, I don't know what I'm going to do with the two of you."

Mary Jo told her in great detail what had taken place, painting vivid word pictures as she described the other woman.

Jessica rolled her eyes. "And you *fell* for it?"

"Fell for what?" Mary Jo cried. "Bambi was all over him. I didn't need anyone to spell it out. I was mortified. Good grief," she said, battling down a sob, "look at me. Last week's vegetable casserole has more hair than I do."

Jessica laughed outright. "Mary Jo, be sensible. The man loves you."

"Yeah, I could tell," she muttered.

"Her name's Barbara, not that it matters. Trust me, she doesn't mean a thing to him."

The doorbell chimed and the two women stared at each other. "Are you expecting company?"

"No."

Jessica lowered her voice. "Do you think it could be Evan?"

On her way to the door, Mary Jo shook her head dismally. "I doubt it."

"Just in case, I'd better hide." Jessica backed out of the room and into the kitchen.

To her complete surprise, Mary Jo found Lois Dryden at the door.

"What happened?" the older woman demanded.

Mary Jo opened the door and let her inside. "Happened?"

"With Evan."

"Jessica," Mary Jo called over her shoulder. "You can come out now. It's a Dryden, but it isn't Evan."

"So, Jessica's here?" Lois said.

"Yes," Jessica said. "But what are *you* doing here?"

"Checking up on Mary Jo. I got a call from Damian. All he said was that he suspected things hadn't gone well with Evan and Mary Jo this morning. He said Mary Jo had phoned and Jessica had hurried out shortly afterward. I want to know what went wrong."

"It's a long story," Mary Jo said reluctantly.

"I tried calling you," Lois explained, "then realized you must still be staying with your family. I was going out, anyway, and I thought this might be an excellent opportunity to meet your mother."

"She's out just now." Mary Jo exhaled shakily and gestured at the sofa. "Sit down, please."

Her parents' house lacked the obvious wealth and luxury of Whispering Willows, but anyone who stepped inside felt immediately welcome. A row of high-school graduation pictures sat proudly on the fireplace mantel. Photos of the grandchildren were scattered about the room. The far wall was lined with bookcases, but some shelves held more trophies than books.

"I understand you went to see Evan this morning," his mother said, regarding her anxiously. "I take it the meeting was something of a disaster?"

"Evan had a *date*," Mary Jo said, glancing sharply at Jessica.

"Hey," Jessica muttered, "all you asked me to do was find out the next time he was going sailing. How was I supposed to know he was meeting another woman?"

"Who?" Lois demanded, frowning.

"Barbara," Mary Jo supplied.

Lois made a dismissive gesture with her hand. "Oh, yes, I know who she is. She's a fashion model who flies in from New York every now and again. You haven't a thing to worry about."

"A fashion model." Mary Jo spirits hit the floor.

"She's really not important to him."

"That may be so," Mary Jo pointed out, "but he certainly looked pleased to see her." Depressed, she slouched down on the sofa and braced her feet against the edge of the coffee table.

Lois's back stiffened. "It seems to me I'd better have a chat with that boy."

"Mother!" Jessica cried at the same moment Mary Jo yelped a protest.

"You promised you weren't going to interfere, remember?" Jessica reminded her mother-in-law. "It only leads to trouble. If Evan wants to make a fool of himself, we're going to have to let him."

"I disagree," Lois said. "You're right, of course, about my talking to him—that would only make matters worse—but we can't allow Mary Jo to let him think he's getting away with this."

"What do you suggest we do?" Jessica asked.

Lois bit her bottom lip. "I don't know, but I'll think of something."

"Time-out," Mary Jo said, forming a T with her hands—a technique she often used with her kindergarten class. "I appreciate your willingness to help, but I'd really like to do my own plotting, okay? Don't be offended, but..." Her words trailed off, and her expression turned to pleading.

Jessica smiled and reached for her hand. "Of course," she said.

Mary Jo looked at Lois, and the woman nodded. "You're absolutely right, my dear. I'll keep my nose out." She reached over and gave Mary Jo a hug.

"Thank you," Mary Jo whispered.

MARY JO DIDN'T HEAR from Evan at all the following week. She tried to tell herself she wasn't disappointed—but of course she was. When it became clear that he was content to leave things between them as they were, she composed a short letter and mailed it to him at his office. After all, it was a business matter.

Without elaborating, she suggested she work for him the next four summers as compensation for the money he'd given her parents.

Knowing exactly when he received his morning mail, she waited anxiously by her phone. It didn't take long. His temporary secretary phoned Mary Jo and set up an appointment for the next morning. By the time she hung up the receiver, Mary Jo was downright gleeful.

The day of her appointment, she dressed in her best suit and high heels, and arrived promptly at eleven. His secretary escorted her into his office.

Evan was at his desk, writing on a yellow legal pad, and didn't look up until the other woman had left the room.

"So, is there a problem?" she asked flatly.

"*Should* there be a problem?"

She lifted one delicate shoulder. "I can't imagine why you'd ask to see me otherwise. I can only assume it has something to do with my letter."

He leaned back in his chair and rolled a gold pen between his palms. "I don't know where you came up with this harebrained idea that I forked over twenty-five thousand dollars to your mother and father."

"Evan, I'm not stupid. I know exactly what you did. And I know why."

"I doubt that."

"I think it was very sweet, but I can't allow you to do it."

"Mary Jo—"

"I believe my suggestion will suit us both nicely. Mrs. Sterling would love having the summers free to travel. If I remember correctly, her husband recently retired, and unless she has the freedom to do as she'd like now and then, you're going to lose her.''

Evan said nothing, so she went on, ''I worked out all right while I was here, didn't I? Well, other than losing that one file, and that wasn't my fault. Naturally, I hope you won't continue trying to make me jealous. It almost worked, you know.''

''I'm afraid I don't know what you're talking about.''

''Oh, Evan,'' she said with an exaggerated sigh. ''You must think I'm a complete fool.''

He arched his thick brows. ''As it happens, I do.''

She ignored that. ''Do you honestly believe you could convince me you're attracted to... to Miss August. I know you better than you think, Evan Dryden.''

His lips quivered slightly with the beginning of a smile, but he managed to squelch it almost immediately.

''Are you agreeable to my solution?'' she asked hopefully.

''No,'' he said.

The bluntness of his reply took her by surprise and her head snapped back. ''No?''

''You don't owe me a penny.''

At least he wasn't trying to get her to believe the money came from Adison Investments.

''But I can't let you do this.''

''Why not?'' He gave the appearance of growing bored. Slumped in his chair, he held the pen at each end and twirled it between his thumb and index finger.

"It isn't right. You don't owe them anything, and if they knew, they'd return it instantly."

"You won't tell them." Although he didn't raise his voice, the tone was determined.

"No, I won't," she admitted, knowing it would devastate her parents, "but only if you allow me to reimburse you myself."

He shook his head. "No deal."

Mary Jo knew he could be stubborn, but this was ridiculous. "Evan, please, I *want* to do it."

"The money was a gift from me to them, sent anonymously with no strings attached. And your plan to substitute for Mrs. Sterling—it didn't work out this summer. What makes you think it will in the future? As far as I'm concerned, this issue about the money is pure silliness. I suggest we drop it entirely." He set the pen down on his desk, as if signaling the end of the conversation.

Silliness. Mary Jo stiffened and reached for her purse. "Apparently we don't have anything more to say to each other."

"Apparently not," he agreed without emotion.

Mary Jo stood and, with her head high, walked out of the office. It wasn't until she got to the elevator that the trembling started.

"ARE YOU GOING to tell me what's troubling you?" Marianna asked Mary Jo. They were sitting at the small kitchen table shelling fresh peas Marianna had purchased from the local farmer's market. Both women quickly and methodically removed the ripe peas from their pods and tossed them into a blue ceramic bowl.

"I'm fine," Mary Jo returned, even though she knew it was next to impossible to fool her mother. After years of raising children and then dealing with grandchildren, Marianna Summerhill had an uncanny knack of knowing when something was right or wrong with any of her family.

"Physically, yes," her mother agreed. "But you're troubled. I can see it in your eyes."

Mary Jo shrugged.

"If I was guessing, I'd say it had something to do with Evan. You haven't seen hide nor hair of him in two weeks."

Evan. The name alone was enough to evoke a flood of unhappiness. "I just don't understand it!" Mary Jo cried. "To hear his mother talk, you'd think he was fading away for want of me."

"He isn't?"

"Hardly. He's dated a different woman every night this week."

"He was mentioned in some gossip column in the paper this morning. Do you know anything about a Barbara Jackson?"

"Yes." Mary Jo clamped her lips together and stewed. If he was flaunting his romantic escapades in an effort to make her jealous, he'd succeeded.

"I imagine you're annoyed."

"'Annoyed' isn't it." She snapped a pea pod so hard, the peas scattered across the tabletop like marbles shooting over a polished hardwood floor. Her mother's smile did nothing to soothe her wounded pride. "What I don't understand," she muttered, "is why he's doing this."

"You haven't figured that out yet?" Marianna asked, her raised voice indicating her surprise. The peas slid effortlessly from the pod to the bowl.

"No, I haven't got a clue. Have *you* figured it out?"

"Ages ago," the older woman said casually.

Mary Jo jerked her head toward her mother. "What do you mean?"

"You're a bright girl, Mary Jo, but when it comes to Evan, I have to wonder."

The words shook her. "What do you mean? I *love* Evan!"

"Not so I can tell." This, too, was said casually.

Mary Jo pushed her mound of pea pods aside and stared at her mother. "Mom, how can you say that?"

"Easy. Evan isn't sure you love him. Why should he be? He—"

Mary Jo was outraged. "Not sure I love him? I can't believe I'm hearing this from my own mother!"

"It's true," Marianna continued, her fingers working rhythmically and without pause. "Looking at it from Evan's point of view, I can't say I blame him."

As the youngest in a big family, Mary Jo had had some shocking things said to her over the years, but never by her own mother. And never this calmly—as if they were merely discussing the price of fresh fruit.

Her first reaction had been defensive, but she was beginning to realize that maybe Marianna knew something she didn't. "I don't understand how Evan could possibly believe I don't love him."

"It's not so hard to understand," Marianna answered smoothly. "Twice you've claimed to love him enough to want to marry him, and both times you've changed your mind."

"But—"

"You've turned your back on him when you were confronted with any resistance from his family. You've never given him the opportunity to answer your doubts. My feeling is, Evan would have stood by you come hell or high water, but I wonder if the reverse is true."

"You make it sound so. . . so simple, but our situation is a lot more difficult than you know or understand."

"Possibly."

"His family is *formidable.*"

"I don't doubt that for an instant," came Marianna's sincere reply. "Let me ask you one thing, though, and I want you to think before you answer. Do you love Evan enough to stand up to opposition, no matter what form it takes?"

"Yes," Mary Jo answered heatedly.

Marianna's eyes brightened with her wide smile. "Then what are you going to do about it?"

"Do?" Mary Jo had tried twice and been thwarted by his pride with each attempt. One thing was certain—Evan had no intention of making this easy for her.

"It seems to me that if you love this man, you're not going to take no for an answer. Unless, of course. . ." Her mother hesitated.

"Unless what?"

"Unless Evan isn't as important to you as you claim."

CHAPTER ELEVEN

MARY JO PUSHED UP the sleeves of her light sweater and paced the floor of her living room. Her mother's comments about the way she'd treated Evan still grated. But what bothered her most was that her mother was right!

No wonder Evan had all but ignored her. He couldn't trust her not to turn her back and run at the first sign of trouble. After all her talk of being older, wiser, and more mature, Mary Jo was forced to admit she was as sadly lacking in those qualities as she'd been three years before. And she was furious.

With herself.

What she needed now was a way to prove her love to Evan so he'd never have cause to doubt her again. One problem was that she had no idea how long it would take for that opportunity to present itself. It might be months—maybe even another three long years. Mary Jo was unwilling to wait. Evan would just have to take her at her word.

But why should he, in light of their past? If he refused, Mary Jo couldn't very well blame him. She sighed, wondering distractedly what to do next.

She could call Jessica, who'd been more than generous with advice. But Mary Jo realized that all Jessica could tell her was what she already knew. Mary Jo needed to talk to Evan herself, face-to-face, no holds barred.

Deciding there was no reason to postpone what had to be done, she carefully chose her outfit—a peach-colored pantsuit with gold buttons, along with a soft turquoise scarf and dangly gold earrings.

When she arrived at his office, Mary Jo was pleasantly surprised to find Mrs. Sterling.

"Oh, my, don't you look lovely this afternoon," the older woman said with a delighted smile. She seemed relaxed and happy; the trip had obviously done her good.

"So do you, Mrs. Sterling. When did you get back?"

"Just this week. I heard about your accident. I'm so pleased everything turned out all right."

"So am I. Is Evan in?"

"I'm sorry, no, but I expect him any time. Why don't you make yourself at home there in his office? I'll bring you some coffee. I don't think he'll be more than a few minutes."

"Thanks, I will." Mary Jo walked into the office and sank onto the sofa. In her determination to see this matter through, she naively hadn't considered the possibility of Evan's being out of the office. And she feared the longer the wait, the more her courage would falter.

She was sipping the coffee Mrs. Sterling had brought her and lecturing herself, trying to bolster her courage, when she heard Evan arrive. Her hands trembled as she set the cup aside.

By the time Evan strolled into the room, still rattling off a list of instructions for Mrs. Sterling, Mary

Jo's shoulders were tensed, as if she was bracing herself for an assault.

His secretary finished making her notes. "You have a visitor," she announced, smiling approvingly in Mary Jo's direction.

Evan sent a look over his shoulder, but revealed no emotion when he saw who it was. "Hello, Mary Jo."

"Evan." She pressed her palms over her knees, certain she must resemble a schoolgirl confronting the principal after some misdemeanor. "I'd like to talk to you, if I may."

He frowned and glanced at his watch.

"Your schedule is free," Mrs. Sterling said emphatically, and when she walked away, she closed the door.

"Well, it seems I can spare a few minutes," Evan said without enthusiasm as he walked behind his desk and sat down.

Mary Jo stood and took the chair across from him. "First I'd like to apologize."

"No," he said roughly. "There's nothing to apologize for."

"But there is," she returned. "Oh, Evan, I've nearly ruined everything."

His eyebrows rose, and his expression was skeptical. "Come now, Mary Jo."

She slid forward in her seat. "It all started that summer we met when—"

"That was years ago, and if you don't mind, I'd prefer to leave it there." He reached for his gold pen, as if he needed to hold on to something. "Rehashing it all isn't going to do either of us any good."

"I disagree." Mary Jo refused to be so easily discouraged this time. "We need to clear up the past. Otherwise once we're married—"

"It seems to me you're taking a lot for granted," he said sharply.

"Perhaps, but I doubt it."

"Mary Jo, I can't see that this will get us anywhere."

"I do," she said hurriedly. "Please listen to what I have to say, and if you still feel the same afterward, then...well, then I'll just say it another way until you're willing to accept that I love you."

His eyebrows rose again. "I have a date this evening."

"Then I'll talk fast, but I think you should know that you aren't fooling me."

"Do you think I'm lying?"

"Of course not. You may very well have arranged an evening with some woman, but it's me you love."

His handsome features darkened in a frown, but she took heart from the fact that he didn't contradict her.

Mary Jo studied her own watch. "How much time do I have before you need to leave?"

Evan shrugged. "Enough."

He wasn't doing anything to encourage her, but that was fine; she knew what she wanted, and she wasn't going to let a little thing like a bad attitude stand in her way.

It took her a few moments to arrange her thoughts and remember what she'd so carefully planned to say. Perhaps that was for the best. She didn't want to sound as if she'd practiced in front of a mirror, although she'd done exactly that.

"You were saying?" Evan pressed.

She nibbled her lower lip. "Yes. I wanted to talk to you about the house."

"What house?" he asked impatiently.

"The one with the seven bedrooms. The one we've discussed in such detail that I can see it clear as anything. The house I want to live in with you and our children."

She noticed that his eyes drifted away from hers.

"I've been doing a lot of thinking lately," Mary Jo continued. "It all started when I was feeling sorry for myself, certain that I'd lost you. I...found the thought almost unbearable."

"You get accustomed to it after a while," he muttered dryly.

"I never will," she said adamantly, "not ever again."

He leaned forward in his chair as if to see her better. "What brought about this sudden change of heart?"

"It isn't sudden. Well, maybe it is. You see, it's my mother. She—"

"Are you sure it wasn't *my* mother? She seems to have her hand in just about everything that goes on between you and me."

"Not anymore." This was something else Mary Jo wanted to correct. "According to Jessica, your mother's been beside herself wondering what's going on with us. We have to give her credit, Evan—she hasn't called or pressured me once. You see, she promised she wouldn't, and your mother's a woman of her word."

"Exactly what did she promise?"

"Not to meddle in our lives. She came to me when I was still in the hospital, and we had a wonderful talk. Some of the problems between us were of my own making. Your mother intimidated me, and I was afraid to go against her. But after our talk, I understand her a little better and she understands me."

She waited for him to make some comment, but was disappointed. From all outward appearances, Evan was merely enduring this discussion, waiting for her to finish so he could get on with his life.

"I'm not Lois's first choice for a daughter-in-law. There are any number of other women who'd be a far greater asset to you and your political future than I'll ever be."

"I'm dating one now."

The information was like a slap in the face, but Mary Jo revealed none of her feelings.

"Above and beyond anything else, your mother wants your happiness, and she believes, as I do, that our being together will provide that."

"Nice of her to confer with me. It seems the two of you—and let's not forget dear Jessica—have joined forces. You're all plotting against me."

"Absolutely not. I've talked to Jessica a number of times, but not recently. It was my mother who helped me understand what was wrong."

"And now *she's* involved." He rolled his eyes as if to say there were far too many mothers interfering in all this.

"All my mother did was show me a few home truths. If anything, we should thank her. She pointed out that you've got good reason to question the strength of my love for you. I was floored that my own mother could suggest something like that. Especially since she knew how unhappy and miserable I've been lately."

The hint of a smile lifted his mouth.

"Mom said if I loved you as much as I claim to, I would have stood by your side despite any opposition. She...she said if our situations had been reversed, you would have stood by me. I didn't, and, Evan, I can't tell you how much I regret it." She lowered her gaze to her hands. "If I could undo the past, step back three years—or even three weeks—I'd do anything to prove exactly how much I love you. I believe in you, Evan, and I believe in our love. Never again will I give you cause to doubt it. Furthermore—"

"You mean there's more?" He sounded bored, as if this was taking much longer than he'd anticipated.

"Just a little," she said, and her voice wavered with the strength of her conviction. "You're going to make a wonderful member of the city council, and I'll do whatever's necessary to see that it happens. It won't be easy for me to be the focus of public attention, but in time, I'll learn not to be so nervous. Your mother's already volunteered to help me. I can do this, Evan, I know I can. Another three or four years down the road, I'll be a pro in front of the cameras. Just wait and see."

He didn't speak, and Mary Jo could feel every beat of her heart in the silence that followed.

"That's all well and good," Evan finally said, "but I don't see how any of it changes things."

"You don't?" She vaulted to her feet. "Do you or don't you love me?" she demanded.

He regarded her with a look of utter nonchalance. "Frankly, I don't know what I feel for you anymore."

In slow motion, Mary Jo sank back into her seat. She'd lost him. She could see it in his eyes, in the way he looked at her as if she was nothing to him anymore. Someone he'd loved once, a long time ago, but that was all.

"I see," she mumbled.

"Now, if you'll excuse me, I have some business I need to attend to."

"Ah..." The shock of his rejection had numbed her, and it took her a moment to get to her feet. She clutched her purse protectively to her stomach. "I...I'm sorry to have bothered you." She drew on the little that remained of her pride and dignity to carry her across the room.

"No bother," Evan said tonelessly.

It was at that precise moment that Mary Jo knew. She couldn't have explained exactly how, but she *knew*. Relief washed over her like the warm blast of a shower after a miserable day in the cold. He loved her. He'd always loved her.

Confident now, she turned around to face him.

He was busily writing on a legal pad and didn't look up.

"Evan." She whispered his name.

He ignored her.

"You love me."

His hand trembled slightly, but that was all the emotion he revealed.

"It isn't going to work," she said, stepping toward him.

"I beg your pardon?" He sighed heavily.

"This little charade. I don't know what you're trying to prove, but it isn't working. It never will. You couldn't have sat by my hospital bed all those hours and felt nothing for me. You couldn't have given my parents that money and not cared for me."

"I didn't say I didn't care. But as you said yourself, sometimes love isn't enough."

"Then I was wrong," she muttered. "Now listen. My mother and yours are chomping at the bit to start planning our wedding. What do you want me to tell them? That the whole thing's off and you don't love me anymore? You don't honestly expect anyone to believe that, do you? *I* don't."

"Believe what you want."

Briefly, she closed her eyes. "You're trying my patience, Evan, but you have a long way to go if you think you can get me to change my mind." She moved closer. There was more than one way of proving her point. More than one way to kick the argument out from under him. And she wasn't going to let this opportunity pass.

She stepped over to his desk and planted both hands on it, leaning over the top so that only a few inches separated their faces. "All right, Dryden, you asked for this."

His eyes narrowed, as she edged her way around the desk. His head followed her movements. He turned in his chair, eyeing her speculatively.

At that moment, she threw herself on his lap, wrapped her arms around his neck and kissed him. She felt his surprise and his resistance, but the latter vanished almost the instant her mouth settled over his.

It'd been so long since they'd kissed. So long since she'd experienced the warm comfort of his embrace.

Groaning, Evan kissed her back. His mouth was tentative at first, then hard and intense. His hold tightened and a frightening kind of excitement began to grow inside her. As she clung to him, she could feel his heart beating as fast as hers, his breathing as labored.

Cradling his face with her hands, she spread eager, loving kisses over his mouth, his jaw, his forehead. "I love you, Evan Dryden."

"This isn't just gratitude?"

She paused and lifted her head. "For what?"

"The money I gave your family."

"No," she said, teasing a corner of his mouth with the tip of her tongue. "But that *is* something we need to discuss."

"No, we don't." He tilted her so that she was practically lying across his lap. "I have a proposition to make."

"Decent or indecent?" she asked with a pretended leer.

"That's for you to decide."

She looped her arms around his neck, hoisted herself upright and pressed her head against his shoulder.

"You'll marry me?" he asked.

"Oh, yes—" she sighed with happiness "—and soon. Evan, let's make this the shortest engagement on record."

"On one condition. You never mention that money again."

"But—"

"Those are my terms." He punctuated his statement with a kiss so heated it seared her senses.

When it ended, Mary Jo had difficulty breathing normally. "Your terms?" she repeated in a husky whisper.

"Do you agree, or don't you?"

Before she could answer, he swept away her defenses and any chance of argument with another kiss. By the time he'd finished, Mary Jo discovered she would have concurred with just about anything. She nodded numbly.

Evan held her against him and exhaled deeply. "We'll make our own wedding plans, understood?"

Mary Jo stared at him blankly.

"This is our wedding and not my mother's—or your mother's."

She smiled softly and lowered her head to his shoulder. "Understood."

They were silent for several minutes, each savoring the closeness.

"Mom was right, wasn't she?" Mary Jo asked softly. "About how I needed to prove that my love was more than words."

"If you'd walked out that door, I might always have wondered," Evan confessed, then added, "You wouldn't have gotten far. I would've come running after you, but I'm glad I didn't have to."

"I've been such a fool." Mary Jo lovingly traced the side of his neck with her tongue.

"I'll give you fifty or sixty years to make it up to me, with time off for good behavior."

The happiness on her face blossomed into a full-blown smile. She raised her head and waited until their eyes met before she lowered her mouth to his. The kiss was long, slow and thorough. Evan drew in a deep, stabilizing breath when they'd finished.

"What was that for?"

"To seal our bargain. From this day forward, Evan Dryden, we belong to each other. Nothing will ever get between us again."

"Nothing," he agreed readily.

The door opened and Mrs. Sterling poked her head in. "I just wanted to check and make sure everything had worked itself out," she said, smiling broadly. "I can see that it has. I couldn't be more pleased."

"Neither could I," Mary Jo said.

Evan drew her mouth back to his and Mary Jo heard the office door click softly shut in the background.

EPILOGUE

Three years later.

"ANDREW, DON'T WAKE Bethanne!" Jessica called out to her four-year-old son.

Mary Jo laughed as she watched the child bend over to kiss her newborn daughter's forehead. "Look, they're already kissing cousins."

"How are you feeling?" Jessica asked, carrying a tall glass of iced tea over to Mary Jo, who was sitting under the shade of the patio umbrella.

"Wonderful."

"Evan is delighted with Bethanne, isn't he?"

"Oh, yes. He reminded me of Damian when you had Lori Jo. You'd think we were the only two women on earth to have ever given birth."

Jessica laughed and shook her head. "And then the grandparents . . ."

"I don't know about you," Mary Jo teased, "but I could become accustomed to all this attention."

Jessica eyed her disbelievingly.

"All right, all right. I'll admit I was a bit flustered when the mayor paid me a visit in the hospital. And it was kind of nice to receive flowers from all those special-interest groups—the ones who think Evan is easily influenced. Clearly, they don't know my husband."

Jessica sighed and relaxed in her lounge chair. "You've done amazingly well with all this. Evan's told Damian and me at least a hundred times or more that you as much as won that council position for him."

Mary Jo laughed off the credit. "Don't be silly."

"You were the one who walked up to the microphone at that rally and said if anyone believed Evan wasn't there for the worker, they should talk to you or your family."

Mary Jo remembered the day well. She'd been furious to hear Evan's opponent state that Evan didn't understand the problems of the everyday working person. Evan had answered the accusation, but it was Mary Jo's fervent response that had won the hearts of the audience. As it happened, television cameras had recorded the rally and her impassioned reply had been played on three different newscasts. From that point on, Evan's popularity had soared.

Bethanne stirred, and Mary Jo reached for her daughter, cradling the infant in her arms.

A sound in the distance told her that Evan and his brother were back from their golf game.

"That didn't take long," Jessica said when Damian and Evan strolled onto the patio. Damian poured them each a glass of iced tea.

Evan took the seat next to his wife. "How long has it been since I told you I loved you?" he asked in a low voice.

Smiling, Mary Jo glanced at her watch. "About four hours."

"Much too long," he said, kissing the side of her neck. "I love you."

"Look at that pair," Damian said to his wife. "You'd think they were still on their honeymoon."

"So? What's wrong with that?" Jessica reached over and squeezed his hands.

He smiled at her lovingly. "Not a thing, sweetheart. Not a damn thing."

Relive the romance....
Harlequin is proud to bring you

A new collection of three complete novels every
month. By the most requested authors, featuring the
most requested themes.

Available in May:

Three handsome, successful, unmarried men are about
to get the surprise of their lives.... Well, better late
than never!

Three complete novels in one special collection:

DESIRE'S CHILD by Candace Schuler
INTO THE LIGHT by Judith Duncan
A SUMMER KIND OF LOVE by Shannon Waverly

Available at you're retail outlet from

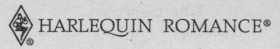

HARLEQUIN ROMANCE®

Coming Next Month!

A new collection from Harlequin Romance

You told us how much you enjoyed The Bridal Collection and our Back to the Ranch series. *Now* Harlequin Romance is bringing you something *new*—KIDS & KISSES—stories that celebrate children. We'll be bringing you one special Romance title every month, beginning in June 1994 (except for December, when we'll have *two* in honor of Christmas!).

Look for these books in 1994:

KIDS & KISSES—celebrating love and children!

KIDSG

Fifty red-blooded, white-hot, true-blue hunks
from every State in the Union!

Look for MEN MADE IN AMERICA! Written by some of
our most popular authors, these stories feature fifty of
the strongest, sexiest men, each from a different state in
the union!

Two titles available every other month at your favorite
retail outlet.

In May, look for:

LOVE BY PROXY by Diana Palmer (Illinois)
POSSIBLES by Lass Small (Indiana)

In July, look for:

KISS YESTERDAY GOODBYE by Leigh Michaels (Iowa)
A TIME TO KEEP by Curtiss Ann Matlock (Kansas)

You won't be able to resist MEN MADE IN AMERICA!

HARLEQUIN®

Don't miss these Harlequin favorites by some of our most distinguished authors!
And now, you can receive a discount by ordering two or more titles!

HT #25551	THE OTHER WOMAN by Candace Schuler	$2.99	☐
HT #25539	FOOLS RUSH IN by Vicki Lewis Thompson	$2.99	☐
HP #11550	THE GOLDEN GREEK by Sally Wentworth	$2.89	☐
HP #11603	PAST ALL REASON by Kay Thorpe	$2.99	☐
HR #03228	MEANT FOR EACH OTHER by Rebecca Winters	$2.89	☐
HR #03268	THE BAD PENNY by Susan Fox	$2.99	☐
HS #70532	TOUCH THE DAWN by Karen Young	$3.39	☐
HS #70540	FOR THE LOVE OF IVY by Barbara Kaye	$3.39	☐
HI #22177	MINDGAME by Laura Pender	$2.79	☐
HI #22214	TO DIE FOR by M.J. Rodgers	$2.89	☐
HAR #16421	HAPPY NEW YEAR, DARLING by Margaret St. George	$3.29	☐
HAR #16507	THE UNEXPECTED GROOM by Muriel Jensen	$3.50	☐
HH #28774	SPINDRIFT by Miranda Jarrett	$3.99	☐
HH #28782	SWEET SENSATIONS by Julie Tetel	$3.99	☐

Harlequin Promotional Titles

#83259	UNTAMED MAVERICK HEARTS (Short-story collection featuring Heather Graham Pozzessere, Patricia Potter, Joan Johnston)	$4.99	☐

(limited quantities available on certain titles)

	AMOUNT	$	
DEDUCT:	**10% DISCOUNT FOR 2+ BOOKS**	$	
	POSTAGE & HANDLING	$	
	($1.00 for one book, 50¢ for each additional)		
	APPLICABLE TAXES*	$	_____
	TOTAL PAYABLE	$	_____
	(check or money order—please do not send cash)		

To order, complete this form and send it, along with a check or money order for the total above, payable to Harlequin Books, to: **In the U.S.:** 3010 Walden Avenue, P.O. Box 9047, Buffalo, NY 14269-9047; **In Canada:** P.O. Box 613, Fort Erie, Ontario, L2A 5X3.

Name: _____

Address: _____ City: _____

State/Prov.: _____ Zip/Postal Code: _____

*New York residents remit applicable sales taxes.
 Canadian residents remit applicable GST and provincial taxes.

HBACK-AJ